MARVEL
MONSTERS UNLEASHED!

THE GRUESOME GORGILLA!

Written by
STEVE BEHLING

MARVEL
Los Angeles
New York

© 2017 MARVEL

All rights reserved. Published by Marvel Press,
an imprint of Disney Book Group. No part of this book may
be reproduced or transmitted in any form or by any means,
electronic or mechanical, including photocopying, recording,
or by any information storage or retrieval system, without
written permission from the publisher. For information address
Marvel Press, 125 West End Avenue, New York, New York 10023.

First Edition, July 2017
10 9 8 7 6 5 4 3 2 1
FAC-020093-17160
Printed in the United States of America

Designed by David Roe
Cover Illustration by Skan Srisuwan

Library of Congress Control Number: 2017905860
ISBN 978-1-368-00248-6

Visit marvelkids.com

THIS LABEL APPLIES TO TEXT STOCK

"Whoever fights monsters should see to it that in the process he does not become a monster."
—Friedrich Nietzsche

"If he lives, there's no telling how dangerous he may be! I pray that we aren't tackling something too big for us to cope with!"
—Stan Lee, *Tales to Astonish* #12

PROLOGUE

HAVE YOU EVER had one of "those days"? You know the kind. The kind of day where you're off doing your own thing one minute, and the next, you find yourself soaring over the Pacific Ocean via repulsor power in a desperate race against time to extinguish an oil-rig fire?

We've all had that kind of day, right?

That's precisely what Tony Stark was thinking from inside the Iron Man armor. Not an hour ago, he had received a distress call from the Coast Guard. Captain America and the other Avengers were elsewhere, engaged in a battle against a subterranean

1

creature called the Minotaur. With the rest of the team busy, and with no one else available to handle the emergency, Stark donned his armor and took to the skies to fight fire with iron.

Fighting an oil-rig fire may not be as fun as fighting the Minotaur, Tony thought to himself. *But it's not nearly as embarrassing as having to tell everyone that I fought a guy who calls himself the Minotaur.*

Up ahead, he could see thick black smoke on the horizon. The oil rig in question belonged to a company called Roxxon. Tony had dealt with Roxxon in the past—they were a shady corporation engaged in lots of shady business. They had even sponsored the creation of some Super Villains, like Orka and Manticore. For all Tony knew, the oil rig might not even really be an oil rig. Maybe it a cover for some ominous experiment? *Nah,* Tony thought. *I'm just being paranoid. But remember what they say:*

Just because you're paranoid doesn't mean they're not out to get you.

Rerouting power reserves to his repulsors, Iron

Man accelerated toward the billowing clouds of black smoke. Soon, the oil rig itself came into view, growing closer with each passing second.

"Iron Man!" came a voice over Tony's communications system. The sudden, unexpected sound startled Tony.

"This is Iron Man, I'm not here right now, so if you could leave your name and number at the—"

"This is the Coast Guard!" said the voice urgently. "We've taken everyone off the rig, except for one person! They refuse to leave! Can you save them?"

Iron Man glanced at the ocean below, and saw two Coast Guard cutters loaded with rescued oil workers. They were heading away from the burning rig, which loomed ahead of the armored Avenger, flames burning brightly as the black smoke billowed upward. The centerpiece of the rig was a tall tower. Activating his visual scanners, Iron Man could make out the figure of a person at the top of the tower, waving their arms.

"First stop, the tower!" Iron Man said. He flew

through the dense smoke and cut the power to his repulsors, coming to a soft landing on a platform atop the tower. He saw a man wearing a white jumpsuit with a full head mask—it immediately struck Tony as odd. The guy looked like he should be working in a laboratory studying strange diseases, not working on an oil rig.

"I hear you don't want to leave!" shouted Iron Man over the din of the fire. "How about you tell me why after I've rescued you?" He extended his right gauntlet toward the man. To Iron Man's surprise, the man backed away.

"They left me!" the man said, nearly hysterical. "They left me! Now he's coming!" He pointed beneath them.

"Who's coming?" Iron Man said sharply. "You mean there's someone else? We've got to get them!"

"They've set him free! We have to leave—now!" the man shouted.

If you're at all confused, imagine how Iron Man must have felt. "Set *what* free?" he shouted, as flames licked the bottom of the platform they were standing on. He moved to grab the man, but as he did so, something swiped Iron Man from behind.

It knocked the Avenger off his feet and onto the hard metal surface. Shaking it off, Iron Man looked up just in time to see an enormous hairy hand reach for him!

Before he could act, the hand grabbed Iron Man. The golden Avenger tried to break free, but the giant hand shook him like a rag doll, leaving Iron Man thoroughly disoriented.

"What in the—" he said as he struggled to get a look at the thing that was giving him the worst case of vertigo since that time he rode the world's largest roller coaster with Hawkeye.

Catching his breath, Iron Man looked quickly at his helmet's heads-up display. The HUD showed exactly what he thought. Whatever was shaking him to pieces was wreaking havoc on his armor's systems. This had to stop, now.

Iron Man fired a few rapid repulsor bursts at the hand, and he heard something shriek. The sound was booming. The hand let go, and Iron Man activated his boot repulsors to take to the air. He flew up and saw the man in white cringing in fear from the giant hand, which was about to grab him.

I don't know what that hand is connected to, Iron Man thought, *but I'd rather not stick around and find out!*

In an instant, he was next to the man in white. He grabbed him by his jumpsuit just before the giant hand could swat him away! Another burst of repulsor fire gave Iron Man a little room to maneuver. He jumped off the platform with the man in white, just as his repulsors kicked on.

Flying away from the burning rig, Iron Man headed toward one of the Coast Guard ships with the man in his arms. "I'm gonna bet there's a pretty interesting story behind all of this," he said to the man. "How about I drop you off and you tell me all about it after I put that fire out?"

Hovering over one of the ships, Tony dropped the man onto the deck. The man was caught by a couple other people wearing similar white jumpsuits.

That's when Tony noticed something else. Something strange.

The Coast Guard boats didn't seem to have any Coast Guard personnel on them. The only people he could see on the ship were the men in white jumpsuits.

An explosion from the oil rig drew Iron Man's attention, leaving him no time to ponder this weird development. He double-timed it back to the oil rig and flew once more into the chaos of growing black smoke and flames. He steeled himself for an attack as he prepped his armor to fight the fire.

To Iron Man's great surprise, there was no sign of the giant thing that had attacked him. It was like it never existed.

How could something so big simply disappear? he thought.

As Iron Man tried to wrap his brain around his circumstances, he activated his gauntlets. Thin streams of an oxygen-depriving chemical sprayed outward. Iron Man worked his way from the tower down to the oil rig proper, aiming for the source of the fire. Slowly, the flames began to die out.

"Worst. Day. Ever," Iron Man said. He tried to reach the Coast Guard boats on his communications system. There was no response.

It was like they never existed.

From aboard one of the Coast Guard boats, a man clad in a white jumpsuit watched the events on the oil rig via holographic monitor. He watched Iron Man slowly, methodically put out the flames on the rig.

"Well?" said a voice over the computer. "How did our little test go?"

The man in white shifted in his seat. "Iron Man didn't know what hit him," he said. "He thought this was a real oil rig. He didn't expect to find a monster waiting for him."

"Brilliant," said the voice. "We're almost ready to unleash it on the world. Is it safe?"

"Arrangements have been made," replied the man

in white. "It is safe. We're en route to you, and will deliver it in a matter of days."

"Good," said the voice. "All goes to plan."

Under the veil of night, you notice things you didn't in the harsh light of day.

Isn't that odd?

Like sounds, for instance. Perhaps precisely because we can't see as well in the dark, our other senses compensate. We rely more on our hearing. Every little sound becomes a symphony to our ears.

The forest overflows with sounds at night. Crickets. Animals. Wind whipping through trees. And anyone who found themselves walking through this particular forest on this particular night would hear them all. But they would be surprised to hear other sounds, sounds that weren't so familiar.

Like the horrible cracking sounds of a pair of hundred-year-old trees being uprooted from the ground. Towering giants that had overlooked the forest were now tossed aside like a child's toys.

Then another unfamiliar sound. An unearthly growl—low, deep. An animal? Perhaps, but no animal anyone had ever heard before. The forest itself rumbled as the growl reverberated through the ground.

An enormous shadow moved beneath the night sky. Taller than the trees.

CHAPTER 1

THE TINY OFFICE was a hot mess. Papers were strewn everywhere, photographs were plastered to the walls, to the desk, to the floor—you name it. It didn't seem like there was even an inch that wasn't covered by something.

Sitting on the floor in the center of it all was Amrita Lakhani. The office belonged to the school newspaper, the *Weekly Caller*. Amrita was the editor of the newspaper, and she took her job very, very seriously. She was hard on her staff, but no harder than she was on herself.

Which wasn't as bad as it seems, considering that Amrita *was* the staff. She was the newspaper's sole editor, writer, and photographer. The other kids at Rosalind Middle School were interested in other extracurricular activities, like soccer, cool robotics courses, book clubs. Rosalind—or Roz, as everyone called it—had awesome extracurriculars. Amrita understood why the other kids liked those things. It wasn't that she *didn't* like them—she did—but she had been bitten by the journalism bug.

On the wall hung pictures of her idols. J. Jonah Jameson, publisher of the *Daily Bugle*. Betty Brant, reporter, and Peter Parker, photographer, who also worked for the storied newspaper. While the other kids in school were memorizing lyrics to their favorite songs or getting ready for sports after school, Amrita was busy reading online newspaper archives. Like her idols, she was obsessed with the truth, and the people's right to know it.

Amrita longed to live in New York City one day and have a job reporting right alongside Betty Brant. She wanted to be right in the middle of the big Super Hero battles, watching Spider-Man tackle

Doctor Octopus, writing down every detail for the eager *Daily Bugle* readers.

Becoming a newspaper reporter had been her dream since she could remember dreaming.

Amrita sifted through a bunch of photos in front of her, until she finally found what she was looking for. She shouted, "Stop the presses!" to nobody at all. The sound didn't even echo in the small, windowless office.

There was a knock at the door. Amrita hoped she hadn't been too loud.

"Everything okay in here?" asked Ms. Malloy as she opened the door. "Did I just hear someone yell 'Stop the presses?' You must have a real scoop!" Ms. Malloy was the faculty advisor to the school newspaper. She was the only person at Roz who seemed as interested in journalism as Amrita. Ms. Malloy entered the small office, causing Amrita to shuffle to one side to give the teacher some room.

"Yeah, everything's great!" Amrita said, excited. "I found the perfect photograph to run with our front-page story!" She thrust the picture directly into Ms. Malloy's face, so close that the teacher couldn't begin to make out what it was. Ms. Malloy smiled, and gently moved Amrita's hands back a little bit so her eyes could see the photo.

"It's . . . cheese," Ms. Malloy said, curious. The photo showed exactly that: an individual slice of cheese in plastic wrap.

"Aha!" Amrita said, jumping up. "That's what they *want* you to think! But it's *not*! It's processed cheese *food*!"

Ms. Malloy's eyes widened, and she nodded, saying nothing.

"This is what they serve to the students at our cafeteria! It's not even real cheese! This is a scoop, Ms. Malloy! I'm gonna blow the lid off this scandal."

"Amrita—" Ms. Malloy interjected.

Amrita kept going. "What do you think of this for a headline—'Cheesegate!'" she said. She waved her hand through the air, as if showing off the headline.

Ms. Malloy didn't say anything, but she didn't have to. Amrita looked at her advisor. Her expression changed from excited to defeated. Her shoulders drooped. "It's a terrible story, I know." Amrita sighed.

"It's not exactly earth-shattering news," Ms. Malloy said, putting an arm around Amrita.

"When am I going to get a great story?" Amrita asked. "I know that every story isn't going to be 'big news,' but I'd settle for ANY news! This school is so dull, nothing ever happens! Why can't it be like New York City? They have Super Heroes in New York City. But I'm not there. I'm here! And I'm stuck solving cheese mysteries!"

Ms. Malloy laughed. "Amrita, you are one of the hardest-working students I have ever met. And you care more about the newspaper than anybody! Keep doing what you're doing. You'll get your story one day. And until then, you are on your way to becoming an excellent reporter."

An excellent reporter, Amrita thought. *Just like Betty Brant.* That's all she wanted to be. But it seemed such a long way off. How was she going to become an excellent reporter in Boringville, USA, population Amrita?

The bell rang, indicating that it was time to move on to the next period. Amrita gathered her books and smiled weakly at Ms. Malloy.

"Don't let it get to you, Amrita," said Ms. Malloy. "You're destined for big things."

CHAPTER 2

THE BEST THING about the bus ride from school to home was that it had to end eventually, Amrita thought. She'd always been an optimist. The bus had so many strikes against it, it wasn't even funny. To begin with, it was noisy and full of kids who didn't seem to know that Amrita was even on the bus to begin with. Plus, it was either too hot inside or too cold, depending on the time of year. It was December now, and the cold of winter was on its way. There hadn't been any snow yet, but you could feel it in the air and in the way the cold seemed to seep through the walls of the bus. Amrita sat in her seat, shivering, watching her breath escape her mouth.

Amrita stared out her window as the bus bumped along the road. How the bus always managed to hit every single pothole was beyond her. Was the bus equipped with some kind of pothole finder?

BUMP!

She flew up an inch or two and landed back on her seat, which had about as much padding as a block of wood. Amrita sighed, and turned back to the window.

What about the school paper? What was she going to do? Had she really tried to convince Ms. Malloy that a front-page story about cheese was a good idea? Sorry, *processed cheese food*? Yikes.

BUMP!

"Earth to Amrita! Come in, Am!"

Amrita whipped her head from the window to look at the person seated right next to her. It was her best friend, Courtney. Courtney was a bit of an outsider, too, just like Amrita. Except it wasn't journalism that she was into—well, not the same kind of journalism as Amrita, anyway. Courtney was really into reading about mysterious animals and creatures. She was always going on about some website that had a lot of monster facts.

Amrita smiled at her friend. "Sorry, Cort," she said, loud enough to be heard over the rumble of the bus. "Just thinking about stuff."

"Stuff. Like . . . let me guess . . . the newspaper?"

"Yes! The newspaper! Cort, I tried to write a story today about cafeteria cheese! Do you have any idea how humiliating that is? What am I doing with my career? It's going nowhere!"

"Your 'career'?" Courtney repeated. "Am, we're, like, twelve. Our career is going to school and hanging out."

"So?" Amrita returned. "Age doesn't have anything to do with it! I want to be a reporter so bad . . . a *real* reporter! Like Betty Brant! Like J. Jonah Jameson!"

"Ugh," said Courtney. "That old guy? The one who hates Spider-Man?" Courtney made an exaggerated frown, and held a finger over her lip, making a mustache. "Blah, blah, blah, Spider-Man!" she said, imitating Jameson. "Blah, blah, blah, menace!"

Amrita started laughing, and soon both girls were cracking up.

"Look, Am, you're too hard on yourself," Courtney said. "Just keep doing what you're doing! If you don't find a great story, I'm sure one will find you."

"Thanks, Cort. You always know what to say."

Amrita turned her attention back to the window and looked outside. The bus was passing by some woods on the way to Amrita's neighborhood. She started to imagine that the rows and rows of towering evergreen trees were skyscrapers and the clunky cars passing by were bright yellow taxicabs. Amrita saw herself in a black power suit, cell phone in one hand and a briefcase in the other, rushing past people on the busy streets of New York City. When she grew up, Amrita was going to be a *somebody*. She just had to be.

BUMP!

The bus hit another pothole. Amrita's head bounced, hitting against the window. "Owwwww," Amrita groaned, looking down at her lap and rubbing her head.

If she had been able to look at the forest for just an instant longer, she would have seen a tall tree shudder and crash to the ground.

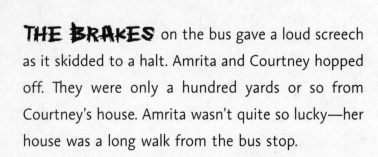

CHAPTER 3

THE BRAKES on the bus gave a loud screech as it skidded to a halt. Amrita and Courtney hopped off. They were only a hundred yards or so from Courtney's house. Amrita wasn't quite so lucky—her house was a long walk from the bus stop.

Amrita let her backpack, heavy with books and homework, drop to the gravel-covered ground below. The cold wind blew, and Amrita zipped up her warm coat to the top. The bus door closed behind her, and the brakes made another screeching sound as the bus pulled away.

"You comin' over?" Courtney asked, jerking

a thumb in the direction of her house. "Cartoons aren't gonna watch themselves, you know."

Amrita shook her head. "Not today. I mean, I'd rather come over and watch ghost shows with you, but I've got a ton of homework. And I have to think of some story for the front page. Something that isn't cheese related." She laughed.

Courtney raised her hands. "Suit yourself! I'm gonna head inside. Talk later?"

"Like I have a choice?" Amrita said as she hefted her backpack over her left shoulder. "You're my best friend! Of course we'll talk later!" With that, she started down the road toward her house.

As she walked on the side of the road, Amrita was struck by how quiet it was. Especially now that the noisy bus was gone. The part of town where she and Courtney lived was out of the way, but really peaceful. The houses were all built right in the woods. It was actually kind of nice being surrounded by nature.

Except for the bugs. Amrita didn't like the bugs.

Maybe that's why she didn't mind the cold weather so much. At least in the cold weather, annoying bugs weren't a problem.

On the walk home, Amrita started thinking about her front-page story for the newspaper again, running possible topics through her mind. As always, her mind started drifting to the future. She thought about what it would be like to work at the *Daily Bugle* in New York City, reporting on all the Super Heroes— and Super Villains. Having her name splashed across the front page, her very own byline—"Story by Amrita Lakhani." That's when she started to have a weird feeling.

You ever have that feeling like you're being watched?

That's the one Amrita had right at that moment. She stopped walking. There was no one around, as far as she could tell. Just the woods to her right, and across the road, more woods. There wasn't anybody around at all.

Weird.

She started walking again, but picked up her pace a little bit. *I'm sure I'm just imagining things,* she thought.

Then she felt it again. Like something was watching her every move. An electric jolt shot up and down the length of her spine. She stopped again, and looked all around.

SNAP!

"What was that?" Amrita shouted, startling herself. "Who's there?" She couldn't see anything for the dense woods. But the loud noise she heard sounded like wood being cracked in two. Like a tree coming down? She stared into the woods closest to her, squinting. The entire forest was dead quiet. *This is so spooky,* Amrita thought. *I don't even see a squirrel or hear any birds.* The air had become still, and her heart was racing now. She could see her breath making small clouds in the cold air. Suddenly, she heard the deafening cracks of hundreds of tiny branches. She spun to her left, her dark hair whipping across her face.

Staring back at her from a bush was a pair of enormous eyes!

Amrita didn't bother to find out who they belonged to.

She turned in the other direction and sprinted back toward Courtney's house.

CHAPTER 4

COURTNEY HAD JUST sat down on her couch with a big glass of lemonade and a bowlful of baby carrots and onion dip. Everything was positioned just so, and she grabbed the TV remote. She pointed the remote at the TV and said, "Let's see what kind of trouble I can get into." And then her front door flew open.

"What in the—" Courtney said as she leaped off the couch. She was shocked to see Amrita standing in her front door, wide-eyed. Amrita threw her backpack right at Courtney as she whirled around, slamming the door shut. Then she slumped against the door with her back and slid down to the floor.

"Doorbell broken?" Courtney asked, clutching Amrita's backpack in her arms.

"Shhhhhhh!" Amrita said, raising an outstretched finger to her mouth in an exaggerated shushing motion. "I might have been followed!"

Courtney set the backpack on the floor and walked over to Amrita. She put both hands on her hips, extending her elbows wide. Amrita grabbed her friend's arm and frantically led her into the kitchen.

"Who would follow you? I mean, who's even around here to follow you? We live in the middle of nowhere!" Courtney walked over to the nearby cabinet and grabbed a cup. She opened the refrigerator, pulled out a pitcher, and poured a glass. "Here, have some lemonade," she said. "It'll calm your nerves."

Amrita was glancing over her shoulders. She ran to the only window in the kitchen and grabbed the curtains, throwing them shut with a *swoosh*. Then she peeked out through an opening she made. It was clear that she was more than a little spooked.

"Well, I'll leave the lemonade here on the counter in case you want it later," Courtney said with a sigh. She walked back to the living room, plopped back on the couch, and grabbed the remote.

"I was just about to catch up on some reality TV," Courtney shouted back at Amrita.

"Don't you care that your best friend could've been killed by who knows what?!" Amrita said, hysterical. She had reappeared behind the couch, her arms up in the air and eyes wide. "And I thought you were gonna watch your ghost shows!"

"Slow down, Am! You know how much sense you're making? All none of it," Courtney replied. "Why don't you take a deep breath and tell me what happened? And yes I *was* gonna watch *Europe's Haunted Cottages*, but a girl can change her mind."

Amrita flung herself on the couch next to Courtney. She took a deep breath, and the words started flowing out of her mouth. "Okay, it's like this.

I was walking home down the road—you know, the road I walk down every day—and it was dull and quiet because we live in the middle of a forest or whatever. And I'm walking and walking and thinking about the school paper and cheese and Super Heroes and my life and how it's over and all that, and then I hear something like a loud *SNAP!* and I'm all like, 'What?' But there's nothing around, at least I can't see anything, you know? I'm looking into the woods and I don't see anything, so I'm a little freaked-out, but then I look harder and then there they are—two of the biggest eyes I've ever seen in my life! And they're staring right back at me, Cort!"

Courtney looked at her friend. "Amrita," she began. "I'm your best friend. Right?"

Amrita nodded rapidly.

"Of course I am. That's why I'm going to tell you that THIS IS SUPER EXCITING! You may have had an encounter with a cryptid!" Courtney held on to Amrita's shoulders and shook her friend.

"I had a what with a who?" Amrita said.

"A cryptid! You had an honest-to-goodness for reals cryptid encounter! I don't believe it. Right here, in our neighborhood!"

Courtney had the biggest, gooniest smile on her face as she stared into Amrita's eyes. She looked like she had just won the lottery or something.

Amrita stared at her friend. At last, she broke the awkward silence. "Pretend I have no idea WHAT a cryptid is, or WHAT you're talking about. Oh wait, you don't have to pretend. Because I don't have any idea what a cryptid is, or what you're talking about!" As soon as the words left her mouth, Amrita felt awful. It wasn't like she hadn't had an opportunity to learn all about cryptids from Courtney. Courtney talked about them all the time. As good a reporter as she was, Amrita had a bad habit of only half listening sometimes.

Ugh . . . I'm such a bad friend, Amrita thought.

"Am, come with me," Courtney said, making a tsk-tsk sound with her mouth. "You are about to take your first step into a larger world." Courtney hopped off the couch and raced up the stairs toward her bedroom.

Amrita looked around the family room nervously to make sure no one was watching her, and ran up the stairs right after her best friend.

CHAPTER 5

COURTNEY'S BEDROOM was a sight to behold. The walls were plastered with posters, featuring all kinds of . . . well, monsters. They had the goofiest-sounding names, like "Tim Boo Ba" and "Spoor" and "Grottu." Some of the creatures were staggeringly huge, dwarfing people and buildings. They all looked mad and mean, like they were ready to rip up a city and eat all the people.

Then there were the books. There were books everywhere! On the bookshelf, sure, but they were also on the floor, on Courtney's desk, and on her bed. There didn't seem to be any surface in the bedroom that wasn't covered with a book of some kind. In its own way, it reminded Amrita of her newspaper office at school. No wonder she and Courtney were best friends. Both girls were completely gung ho about their interests. They immersed themselves into whatever they liked. They were also both pretty messy.

When Amrita got to Courtney's room, her friend was already on the bed, shoving a pile of books onto the floor. They landed with a loud thud. Courtney then patted the bed, indicating for Amrita to sit next to her.

"Lesson time!" Courtney shouted, clearly excited. She had her tablet computer in her hands, and flipped open the cover. Her hand pressed the screen as Amrita plopped down next to her on the bed. "Cryptids," she began, sounding like an overly earnest teacher. "What are they? Creatures! Creatures that have not yet been proven to exist."

Amrita glanced at her friend, nodding, but couldn't take her eyes off the sheer number of books that populated Courtney's room. "Seriously,

Cort. How many books do you have? And they're all on the same subject!" Amrita chided. Then she made a face. "I wasn't listening, was I?"

Courtney tapped the edge of the tablet impatiently, waiting for a page to load. "First of all, they are NOT all on the same subject. Some of these books are about lake-dwelling cryptids. There's a whole section about ancient cryptids that have been revived in the present day. I even have a book all about the Avengers fighting Fin Fang somebody or other. I could go on, but you get the point."

Amrita nodded again, sheepishly. She really was trying to listen. But it was all so fantastic! Monsters—like, *for real* monsters. Was it possible that such things really existed?

"Aha!" Courtney yelled, startling Amrita. "Take a look at this!" She thrust the tablet into Amrita's hands and pointed at the screen.

"*Tales to Astonish*?" Amrita said. "This is the website that you're always talking about."

Courtney grinned. "Indeed! You should totally check it out. Maybe we can find out something about those big, creepy eyes that were watching you from the woods! Like, what those eyes are connected to!"

Amrita shuddered. Part of her was scared, almost too scared—did she really want to know what lurked in those woods? But then another part of her, the reporter, told her that this was a big story. Maybe *the* story.

Courtney hit the Message Board button on the *Tales to Astonish* site, and the page loaded. Amrita looked over Courtney's shoulder at some of the topics: Land Cryptids, Sea Cryptids, Myths & Monsters, Super Heroes & Cryptids . . . it all seemed kind of unbelievable to Amrita. But Courtney was her best friend—they had known each other since first grade! She knew Courtney was really smart, and wouldn't just believe something without doing her research. Maybe there was something to this . . . ?

"I'm e-mail buddies with a kid from a couple of towns over: Ben," Courtney said, as Amrita scrolled through the various topics. "He's super into this site, too. We exchange a lot of messages about all the interesting stuff on *Tales to Astonish*. Cryptids.

Y'know, weird creatures. Monsters." Courtney made a spooky face, and Amrita laughed.

"This is an awful lot to take in, Cort," Amrita said, riveted to the screen. "I mean, real monsters?"

"Sure! The Hulk's kind of a monster, sort of, isn't he? You believe in him, don't you?"

"Well, yeah," Amrita said, shrugging her shoulders. "But that's because the Hulk is real. He's one of the Avengers, for crying out loud! We've seen him on TV. He's had his picture taken with Tony Stark! Not believing in the Hulk is like not believing in processed cheese food."

"So, same thing with monsters! Ben was posting recently about a monster—like, a real monster. That he and his sister found. It's called the Glop!"

"Get out. They did NOT find a monster! And 'the Glop'? Really? What kind of a name is that?"

"First of all, my house, so I don't have to get out—you do. Second, they did so! And third, yeah, it's really called the Glop! I don't name the monsters, Am, I just talk about 'em. Ben has a whole thread about it. Here, take a look!" Courtney clicked on the thread, and Amrita started to read. She couldn't believe it at first. The thread talked all about a weird statue covered in some kind of goo that suddenly came to life and started chasing after a kid and his sister. The post made it sound like the goo was from another planet—an alien!

As Amrita read, she noticed that a lot of the posts in the thread were from a "Kid Kaiju." The name sounded familiar, but she couldn't quite place it.

"Who's Kid Kaiju?" Amrita asked innocently enough.

"Who's Kid Kaiju?" Courtney said, jumping up, now standing on her bed. She gave Amrita a look that said, *I can't believe you're asking me this question.*

"Who's Kid Kaiju?! He's, like, the main cryptid kid!" Courtney said. "He knows everything about monsters! Everything! How is it remotely possible that you don't know who Kid Kaiju is, Am?! I talk about him all the time. ALL. THE. TIME."

Amrita grimaced. "I don't know?" she answered. "Bad listener?"

"You have a lot to learn, and you need new ears,"

Courtney said, shaking her head. "But the first thing you're going to do is make a post."

"I am?" Amrita asked. "Wait. What. On *Tales to Astonish*?"

"Definitely! Do you want to find out what those big freaky eyes belonged to?"

"Not really."

"Of course you do! You're a journalist, aren't you? You want to know the truth, don't you? Here, I'll help you!" With that, Courtney started to type. Amrita knew there was no talking her friend out of it. So she started talking, telling her tale again, as Courtney made a new thread on *Tales to Astonish*.

CHAPTER 6

SCHOOL DIDN'T START until 8:30 a.m. So the halls were completely empty when Amrita showed up at 7:30. She liked getting to school before any of the other students. It gave her time to think and plan what she was going to write about. Amrita opened her locker and chucked her backpack inside. Then she grabbed a notebook and headed straight for the newspaper office. It was a little generous, calling it an office, Amrita thought. All the other clubs in school had designated meeting places, like the gym, or the cafeteria, or the library. But those clubs needed the space because they had a lot of members. There was only one member of the school newspaper—Amrita.

She came to a nondescript wooden door with a piece of paper taped to it. On the piece of paper were the words THE WEEKLY CALLER written in black permanent marker. When she opened the door, Amrita regarded the room. But it wasn't a room, she thought. It was a closet. Like, literally a closet. It had been a custodian's supply closet until Ms. Malloy fought to convert the space for the school newspaper. *Oh well,* Amrita thought. *Closet or no, it's home.*

"All right people, let's get to work!" she said, to no one. Even though she was the only person who worked on the newspaper, Amrita liked to imagine she had a big staff. It made things a little less lonely.

Sitting down at her computer, Amrita started to type a new story. No more processed cheese food stories for her. This one was all about her strange experience from yesterday. She was going to tell everyone in school about it! Maybe this could be her big scoop.

Amrita wanted to make sure she got every last detail right, so she logged into talestoastonish.com. Courtney had done an awesome job of transcribing everything Amrita had told her, and she wanted to check her notes. Amrita found her thread, and was surprised to see that she actually had a response!

 KidKaiju:
You're onto something. Something big. And I think I may know exactly what it is . . . Gorgilla.

The post was signed *Kid Kaiju*. The guy that Courtney was telling her about! Right off the bat, Courtney was talking with the monster expert himself. Maybe Amrita could get an exclusive interview for the newspaper! Excited, Amrita bit her lip and started to type a response:

 Amrita:
What do you think I'm onto? How big? Who's Gorgilla?

She hit Post, and went back to work on her article. The idea that maybe she could get Kid Kaiju on the record to talk about this monster stuff was too exciting. Who would have thought? Her fingers flew across the keyboard. The story seemed to write itself!

As Amrita worked, she kept the web browser open behind her article. She wanted to be able to refer back to her account of yesterday's big-eyed monster encounter on *Tales to Astonish*. She was surprised when she saw the thread updated—Kid Kaiju had just posted another response!

KidKaiju:
Gorgilla's a what, not a who. And if he's in your town, you're gonna need help.

Amrita gulped. That didn't sound good. She bit her lower lip and typed a quick response.

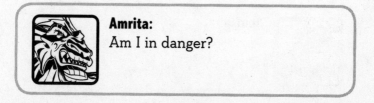

Amrita:
Am I in danger?

Then she stopped work on the article and ran a search on *Tales to Astonish*.

"All right, website all about weird monsters," Amrita said out loud. "Show me everything you have on Gorgilla. . . ."

CHAPTER 7

"DOES THIS BUS even have walls?" Courtney asked as she hugged herself tightly. She was wearing a big puffy coat, along with a scarf, hat, and mittens. Amrita had to wonder if there was even a person inside all those clothes. But her friend was right. The bus was colder than ever on the ride home.

Colder, and finding even more potholes than usual, Amrita observed, as—

BUMP!

—the bus hit another one, sending her off her seat and a few inches into the air.

But Amrita didn't really care about the cold or the potholes. Not today, anyway. She was beyond excited because that week's edition of the *Weekly Caller* had gone to press and was now in the hands of everyone on the bus!

Well, some people's hands, Amrita thought. A couple of kids in the seat in front of her were reading the newspaper out loud, and Amrita eavesdropped:

"Come on, let me read it!"

"Oh, you're gonna love it. Apparently there's a giant monster on the loose!"

"What? Did she really write that?"

"Ha! Yeah! She says it's called 'Grogiller'!"

Amrita snapped and stood up on the bus, leaning over her seat. The two kids were shocked by the sudden invasion of their space, and even more shocked when Amrita launched into a rant.

"It's 'Gorgilla,' not 'Grogiller'!" she started. "What even IS a Grogiller? That makes no sense! And yes, it's all true, and it really happened, and I'm investigating this story all the way! I'm gonna prove that Gorgilla is real!"

"We were just kidding around!" one of the kids said.

"Yeah," said another kid. "Like, just joking! We didn't mean anything by it!"

Amrita showed her teeth and growled.

"Am!" Courtney hush-whispered. She grabbed her friend by her shoulders and pulled her back down into the seat. "You need to chill. Look, they're just being ridiculous. You know what you know, and Kid Kaiju does, too. Just focus on that."

Amrita grumbled. "It's just . . . I'm sure I look like a dope! Everyone's making fun of me."

"So? Who cares? Stick to your guns! Isn't that what a journalist does? Goes after the truth no matter what?" Courtney said, trying to lift her friend's spirits.

"Yeah, you're right," Amrita said. "My gut is telling me that there's something to this story. There has to be!"

BUMP!

The bus rode over another pothole.

"Then what are you gonna do about it, Am?" Courtney prodded.

"I am gonna keep on investigating and follow my

gut!" Amrita yelled, above the sound of the noisy bus's engine and tires.

Everyone around them turned to stare at Amrita.

"Right after I die of embarrassment," she said, shrinking into her seat.

Courtney put a hand on her friend's shoulder. "It could be worse," she said.

"How is that possible?" Amrita said, looking out the bus window.

"You could be stuck writing that cheese story."

Amrita laughed.

CHAPTER 8

THE BUS DROVE off, leaving Amrita and Courtney standing on the street alone. Courtney started to walk toward her house.

"Well, I'll see you tomorrow, Am," Courtney said, throwing her friend a wave good-bye.

"Where do you think you're going?" Amrita asked.

"Uh . . . home? To do my homework? Watch *Paranormal Adventures*? Read about monsters?" Courtney replied.

"No, no, no," Amrita said, taking her friend by the arm and yanking her toward the road. "All of those things can wait. Right now, you are coming with me, and we are heading into the woods."

"We are?" Courtney said, pulling back a little bit.

"Yes, we are! We're going to find proof of this thing, this . . . Gorgilla!"

Courtney shook her head back and forth, faster than Amrita had ever seen her shake her head before.

"I am NOT going into the woods in search of Gorgilla. That is the exact opposite of what I'm going to do. Because what I'm going to do is going to look an awful lot like me walking inside my house!" Courtney turned, and started to walk/run toward her home. Amrita followed.

"What is going on? Yesterday, you were the one who was all like, 'Yay, cryptids!' And now you're chickening out?"

"Chickens have excellent self-preservation instincts," Courtney shot back.

"They do not!" Amrita replied. "Come on. Just think of it. If we do find proof of Gorgilla's existence, do you have any idea how huge that will be? Besides, you told me to follow my gut. Don't you want me to be a real journalist and get my scoop?"

Amrita batted her eyes at Courtney, looking as innocent and needy as she could.

Courtney growled. "Oh, all right!" she said, turning back around and walking over to Amrita. "Fine, let's go get Gorgilla! Just make sure I'm back home in time for dinner."

Amrita clapped and jumped in the air, then the two walked away from Courtney's house and down the road, toward the woods.

"That was a good guilt trip back there," Courtney said as she walked through a stand of trees.

Amrita nodded. "Yeah, it was. I learned it from my mom. She's like the queen of guilt trips." Amrita slowly came to a stop as a sad realization passed over her face. "Was. I mean she was, like, the queen of guilt trips."

Courtney put her hand on her best friend's shoulder. Amrita looked over at Courtney, her eyes clouded in memory. "I can't believe it's been two years since I last saw her."

"And your dad still won't tell you what happened?" Courtney asked. The two best friends had become like sisters when Amrita's mom went missing two summers ago. When Amrita needed a distraction from all of the chaos, Courtney was there for her.

The entire town came together to try and find her. For weeks, they searched the woods but they found nothing. No clothes. No note. No clues. The police were dumbfounded. Nothing like this had ever happened in the tiny town, and it frightened everyone. The day Mrs. Kali Lakhani went missing was the last day anyone left their front doors unlocked.

Amrita thought for a moment and then looked straight ahead. "My dad could never explain how someone could just up and vanish like that." Amrita gave her friend a small, tired smile and started walking again. "Imagine if I cracked that case. Now THAT would be the biggest scoop of my career."

The woods were quiet, and there was still daylight. It was about 4:00 p.m., so that meant the girls had about another hour of sun so they could see their way through the woods. After that, darkness would fall.

They walked along the dirt, combing through the area where Amrita had seen those two huge eyes the day before. So far, they saw nothing. Just some giant potholes in the dirt.

Then another pothole.

And another.

"Since when are there potholes in the woods?" Courtney asked.

That didn't sit right with Amrita, and she took a step back to examine one of the "potholes." It was gigantic. Much bigger than any "pothole" she had ever seen on the street. This one looked enormous. It was almost big enough for Amrita and Courtney to lie down inside!

That's when Amrita noticed something else really weird about the "potholes."

They were shaped like footprints.

Colossal footprints.

CHAPTER 9

"**HOLY . . . !**" Courtney shouted. "That's a footprint, Am! Like the kind of print a foot makes!"

Amrita couldn't believe it. But there it was, plain as day. A ginormous footprint in the dirt! She whipped out her cell phone and snapped a few pictures. Then she slapped Courtney on the arm.

"Proof!" Amrita shrieked. "Actual proof! Courtney, this is huge!"

"Like those footprints."

"Yeah, exactly! Come on, we have to follow these and see where they lead!"

"I was afraid you were gonna say that," Courtney

said. As Amrita ran off into the woods following the footprints, Courtney followed her. Reluctantly.

The girls raced through the woods as they followed the giant footprints. Sometimes they were running alongside them, other times right into and out of them. The footprints led them away from the road and farther and farther into the woods. The sun was starting to fade, making its way toward the horizon. There wasn't much daylight left.

Soon it would be dark.

And the girls would be alone in the woods with whatever had made those giant footprints.

Gorgilla?

"What's that?" Amrita said softly as she reached a clearing in the woods. She ducked behind a tree and motioned for Courtney to join her. An uncomfortable, spooky feeling welled up inside her.

"What's what?" said Courtney in her normal tone of voice.

Amrita shot her a look. "Keep your voice down!

Look!" She pointed into the clearing, and Courtney saw it. It was a huge white dome. The thing had to be the size of an airplane hangar. Bigger. It looked big enough to hold a S.H.I.E.L.D. Helicarrier, Amrita thought. But what was it? Where had it come from? Who put it there? And what was it doing in the middle of the woods in her town?

"Seriously weird, Cort," Amrita said. "This can't be just a coincidence. This place must have something to do with those footprints . . . and whatever made them."

Then they saw something move. It looked like a person, wearing an all-white jumpsuit, with a helmet and face mask—like a containment suit of some kind. Like the ones that scientists were always wearing in zombie movies when they were trying to find a cure for the infection.

Maybe it was watching too many horror movies at Courtney's house, but that last observation didn't make Amrita feel any better.

The person in white had come out of an octagonal

opening in the dome. Then another person emerged. Then another.

What was going on out here in the middle of nowhere? Who were these people? They looked like something out of a science-fiction movie. They sort of reminded Amrita of A.I.M.—a group of rogue scientists who had fought Captain America about a jillion times. Except the A.I.M. guys wore yellow jumpsuits, and had helmets that kind of looked like beekeeper masks.

The girls watched as they saw a white jeep drive toward the dome, carrying two more people in white suits. The jeep came to a halt by the dome's opening, and they jumped out. They beat a path through the overgrown brush toward the opening, and the other people in white suits joined them. "What are they doing?" Courtney whispered, almost angry. These creepy strangers in white suits were using the town to conduct some weird research projects right under everyone's noses. It was insulting. "Who do these people think they are?"

"Whoever they are, what they're doing has to be illegal. It's too weird not to be," Amrita said.

"What if it's the government. What if they're doing government experiments?" Courtney said. "I saw this one episode of *Alien Archaeologists* that said that the government was planting extraterrestrial plant life in the middle of—"

Suddenly, Amrita clasped her hand over Courtney's mouth.

"Shhh! They'll hear us."

With her hand still over Courtney's mouth, Amrita watched as the people in white jumpsuits cleared away the brush until they finally made it to the dome. There wasn't a door, but with the wave of someone's badge, one quickly appeared. The people in white filed inside one by one, until the last person closed the door securely behind him. Then, once again, there was no one. Just Amrita and Courtney.

Suddenly, there was a deafening . . .

SNAP!

Amrita jerked her head backward to see an ancient, gnarled tree falling right toward them!

58

CHAPTER 10

THE TREE FELL HARD and slammed into the ground. Along the way, it took out some other, smaller trees, some branches, and some plants. Anything in its path was heading toward Flat City.

But not Amrita and Courtney. They had managed to roll out of the way at the last possible second. They were now both covered in dirt, but at least they hadn't been flattened by a tree. They looked at each other, then looked at the stump of the tree that had almost crushed them. It was a clean break. Like something had pushed the tree over. Deliberately.

How big would something have to be to knock over a tree? Amrita thought.

They heard a rustling sound.

"Move it!" Amrita shouted, and the two girls got to their feet and sprinted out of the woods and into the clearing. The girls ran and ran, until they were about halfway between the edge of the woods and the dome. They slumped to the ground as adrenaline coursed through them.

"I knew going into the woods with you was a bad idea!" Courtney said, huffing and puffing. "I could be safe at home watching *Paranormal Investigations* right now, instead of conducting one of my own!"

"Something just tried to kill us!" Amrita said.

"Oh, you think?" Courtney responded sarcastically.

It was darker than before, as the sun slipped past the horizon line. Lights from within and around the dome grew brighter, illuminating the clearing. The girls caught their breath, and that's when they noticed that some of the lights were moving.

Searchlights.

"Searchlights!" Amrita shouted. "They must have heard all that commotion!"

"They?" Courtney said as the girls got to their feet. "Who they?"

"Them they!" Amrita said, pointing at the door of the dome that had just opened. Several people in white containment suits ran outside as the searchlights swung right on the girls!

"Over there!" shouted one of the people, as two others hopped into the jeep. They were heading right for Amrita and Courtney! The girls started to run back toward the woods.

A voice boomed over a loudspeaker. "Halt! You two! You're trespassing on private property!"

"Oh, man," Courtney said, running. "Not only does something try to kill us with a tree, but now we're trespassers? *So* not good!"

"Keep running, Cort!" Amrita said, pumping her legs. "We have to make it back into the woods before those creeps catch up to us! It's dark enough. . . . I think we can lose them in the woods!"

Amrita could feel her heart in her throat. A giant lump had formed there, and she could barely swallow.

That's when she realized how afraid she really was.

The girls ran as the jeep quickly followed, catching up to them. The engine sounded closer and closer, the jeep's headlights illuminating the path in front of them.

"Don't let them get away!" said one of the creeps.

"They've seen too much!" said another.

At last, they reached the edge of the woods. The girls dived inside, and kept on running. Smaller branches broke as they pushed their way past tree after tree, moving fast as they could.

The girls turned around just in time to see the jeep come to a sudden stop at the edge of the woods. The people in the white suits got out and started looking around.

"That was close," Courtney said, as she started to run again.

Amrita was just about to turn and run with her friend, when she heard it. Like something hitting metal. Suddenly, the lights on the jeep went out. There were screams. The screams were coming from the people dressed in white.

Amrita whirled around, and caught a glimpse of what was happening behind her in the darkness. She saw a giant hairy hand take a swipe at the jeep, reducing it to pieces.

Amrita turned, ran, and didn't look back.

CHAPTER 11

AMRITA AND COURTNEY trudged along the side of the road in darkness. They were cold, tired, sweaty, dirty, and scared out of their wits. Amrita glanced at the time on her cell phone as she typed. It was 6:45 p.m., and she had about a bajillion missed calls and voice mails from her dad that she hadn't bothered to return.

She was dead.

"I'm so dead," Courtney said, as if she was reading Amrita's mind. "I should have been home for dinner forever ago. I *told* you it was a bad idea to go out looking for that thing! Remember when I told you it was a bad idea? I meant it!"

Amrita put an arm around her friend. "Look, if it makes you feel any better, I'm just as dead as you are. My dad is going to kill me for coming home so late without so much as a phone call."

Courtney gave her a look as if to say, *How is* that *supposed to make me feel better?*

Slowly, the fear faded from Amrita. All the excitement of the afternoon started to bubble up inside her, and she could now barely contain her enthusiasm. "But come on! This is a *real* story! Strange happenings in the woods! A monstrously huge hand, which, presumably, is connected to a monstrously huge creature! Mysterious dudes in weird white suits. A secret hideout in the middle of nowhere! We trespassed! We almost got captured!"

It was only then that Amrita realized they had stopped walking, and that she had grabbed her friend by the shoulders and was shaking her. Amrita gave Courtney a sheepish grin and let go.

"Yeah," Courtney said in a serious tone. "That's right. We almost got captured."

The pair started to walk again.

"Sorry," Amrita said. "I didn't mean to get you in trouble. But something finally happened in our boring old town! This is too amazing!"

Courtney bit her lip, a nervous habit she had. "I mean, it was pretty amazing. Did we really just come face-to-face with a cryptid?"

"More like face-to-hand, but yeah, I think we did! What else could it have been?" Amrita answered as she continued to type on her phone. "I'm posting everything to *Tales to Astonish!*"

Amrita typed quickly, posting the photograph of the giant footprint, along with a message:

Amrita:
Things are getting weirder. Found these in the woods outside of town. What do you make of them? And wait until I tell you the rest. Saw a giant hairy hand! Weird guys in white! A weird lab or something!

Courtney cocked her head and gave her friend a funny look. "Since when do *you* have a *Tales to Astonish* account?"

Amrita smiled, not taking her eyes off the screen. "Since I saw a giant monster! And since I signed up last night, after I got back from your place, silly!"

"It really is kind of awesome," Courtney said, kicking a rock as she walked.

"Mmm-hmmm," Amrita replied.

"And when we get home, we really are kind of dead."

"Mmm-hmmm."

It was about five minutes later when the girls reached Courtney's house. The lights were on outside. Her mom was standing on the porch, arms crossed. Courtney took a big gulp. "See you tomorrow at school, Am," Courtney said as she walked toward the house. "If they let me out of prison."

Amrita gave a nervous laugh and waved at Courtney's mom. She returned the wave with a frown.

Starting down the road toward her house, Amrita couldn't stop thinking about what happened. What exactly was going on in her small town? Who were those strange people in the white suits? They weren't the police, that was for sure. Government, maybe? Something else? Real live bad guys? What were they doing back there in the woods? This was such a big story, and she needed answers to her questions.

Several minutes passed, and Amrita saw her house. Her dad was standing outside with the lights on, just like Courtney's mom had been waiting for her. Amrita took a deep breath, ready for the confrontation with her dad.

But honestly, she wasn't really worried. More than anything else, she was excited! She couldn't wait to run up to her room and check *Tales to Astonish*. Maybe Kid Kaiju had already seen her post. He could probably answer Amrita's questions. She was all set to write the biggest story of her newspaper career!

CHAPTER 12

THE NIGHT HAD COME and gone, and miraculously, Amrita had survived. Her dad was angry as anything, of course, but only because he had no idea where his daughter was. Amrita was usually so good about calling whenever she might be late. After her mom went missing, Amrita's once fun and laid-back dad was now constantly worried about her. Amrita apologized up and down, and told him that she and Courtney had been working on a project for school, and had totally lost track of time. She must have accidentally turned off her cell phone, and that's why she didn't get any of his calls.

Aside from the cell phone part, the story was

totally true as far as Amrita was concerned. She and Courtney had most *definitely* been working on a school project—Amrita's big news story for the school paper! And truthfully, they did lose track of time. That's what happens when you're wandering around the woods and giant creatures and weird people in white suits are chasing after you.

Still, it felt wrong. Amrita didn't like keeping things from her dad. They had been through too much together. The two of them had never had any secrets between them before. Amrita resolved that as soon as she broke her big story, she would tell her dad everything. But would he believe her? Would anyone believe what she and Courtney had experienced?

The class bell rang, and Amrita snapped out of her daydream. It was 9:00 a.m., and the first class of the day was Literature. Amrita liked it because, well, she loved to read and write. But Ms. Malloy was her Literature teacher, too. That made the class more fun. She *got* Ms. Malloy, and Ms. Malloy got Amrita.

"All right, everyone, quiet down," Ms. Malloy

said. "No doubt you're all talking about seeing that new Super Hero, Falcon, who was spotted just a few towns over. Check that out on your own time. You're on Malloy time now."

"The Falcon?" Amrita asked in a voice that was way too loud, causing all eyes in the room to fall on her. She shrank back in her seat, but only a little. "You mean like, guy-with-wings-under-his-arms-who's-also-an-Avenger Falcon? *That* Falcon? Where was he? What happened? What did I miss?"

"Relax, Scoop," said one of the students. Everyone laughed. The other kids knew how much Amrita wanted to be a reporter. Sometimes they teased her because of it. It didn't really bother Amrita much. It was more annoying than anything else.

"That's enough," Ms. Malloy said, firmly. She looked at Amrita. "You know how it is, heroes are popping up all over all the time. Apparently Falcon went soaring through our area last night on his way to save some lives. Something to do with 'the Night People,' whoever they might be."

Amrita was disappointed. True, she was working

on her own big story, the biggest of her life. But man, a chance to see Falcon? To find out what he was up to? To investigate the Night People, whoever they were? To write *that* story? Now more than ever, Amrita was sure that she was destined to be a reporter. Perhaps the story she was working on would be her ticket to a job at the *Daily Bugle*! She could see it now—J. Jonah Jameson himself assigning her to cover a big story. Maybe Peter Parker would be her photographer!

"Open your books to chapter eighteen," Ms. Malloy said, walking up to the whiteboard. "Today, we're going to talk about fate."

There was too much excitement coursing through Amrita's veins, and she found her mind wandering. All that talk of Falcon and thinking about the Avengers had distracted her for just a second. She had almost forgotten about her own mystery! When she left for school that morning, there had been no response yet from anyone on *Tales to Astonish*. So she logged back on and wrote all about the strange encounter in the woods, the bizarre finding of the dome in the middle of nowhere, the people in the white suits, the jeep getting smashed—all of it. Oh yeah, and the big furry hand, too. She made sure every detail was captured for *Tales to Astonish* readers. Especially Kid Kaiju.

As Ms. Malloy spoke to the class about fate, Amrita looked out the classroom window. Her mind was wandering again. Across the street, she saw a plain, unmarked white van. Standing behind the white van on the curb were two people dressed in white suits.

They were exactly the same suits that the people who threatened Amrita and Courtney were wearing last night.

A jolt ran up Amrita's spine. What were they doing here? Had they been following her? How? Did they know who she was? What were they going to do to her? Her breathing sped up, and Amrita could hear her own heartbeat thrumming in her ears. She thought she heard her name being called, but it seemed so distant, so far away.

"Amrita!" Ms. Malloy called, looking a little

annoyed. Amrita whipped her head to look at her and realized that her teacher must have been saying her name several times before she noticed.

"I'm sorry, Ms. Malloy, I was just—"

That's when she noticed a boy around her age standing in the door of the classroom. He had a big sketchbook tucked under one arm. He didn't look familiar. Roz was a small school, and Amrita pretty much knew what everybody looked like.

"Amrita, I've been calling you! This young man says the principal wants to see you. What's your name again?" Ms. Malloy said, turning toward the boy in the doorway.

"Um, Kei," he said. "New kid." He looked nervous, fidgety. Like he really wanted to be anywhere other than here. He ran a hand through his shaggy black hair.

"Far be it from me to stand in the way of our fair principal," Ms. Malloy said. "Come back when you're finished, Amrita. Be prepared to answer some questions about fate."

Amrita got up from her seat and looked out the window once more.

The white van and the people in white suits were gone. It was like they were never there.

Maybe she had imagined the whole thing?

Amrita exited the classroom, giving Ms. Malloy a weak smile, and started to walk down the hallway with Kei.

Once the classroom door was closed, Kei grabbed Amrita's arm and whispered, "Come with me if you want to save Gorgilla!"

CHAPTER 13

WHEN SOMEONE you've never seen before in your life tells you to go with them if you want to save a monster, should you go?

That's the thought that was buzzing through Amrita's mind at that exact moment. Everything was happening so fast. Less than a minute ago, she was sitting in class, minding her own business. Now everything seemed to be falling apart.

Who was this Kei person? How did he know about Gorgilla? Or Amrita, for that matter? How did he know where to find her? Did he have anything to do with those weirdos in white who disappeared just as quickly as they appeared?

What exactly was going on?

And that's when she realized . . .

"Kid Kaiju?" she said, looking at Kei. The boy with the messy black hair and orange hoodie looked at Amrita, smiled shyly, and gave his head a sharp nod.

"Less talking, more running," he said as he sped off down the hallway. Without missing a step, Amrita followed right behind him. Her feet pounded on the tiles beneath her.

"Hey! You two! Stop right there!"

Both Kid Kaiju and Amrita looked over their shoulders. Behind them, at the other end of the hallway, they saw the people in the white suits. They weren't wearing their containment masks but had on dark sunglasses instead.

"Really, run!" Kid Kaiju shouted as the people in white took off after them.

Amrita took Kid Kaiju's hand as she raced ahead, pulling him along with her. "That's one way to get out of class!"

० ० ०

Amrita flung open two doors marked EXIT that opened out into an alleyway behind the school. There was a large green dumpster full of trash, and several smaller blue recycling bins near it. She and Kei spilled out through the doors, and slammed them shut. He looked around for something to jam through the door handles.

"Hand me that mop!" he said to Amrita. She grabbed a mop that was standing near the door and tossed it to Kid Kaiju. He shoved the mop through the door handles. Anyone on the inside trying to push out would have a hard time opening the doors now.

"Keep running and don't look back," Kid Kaiju said, and Amrita did exactly that.

"Who ARE those guys?" Amrita asked as they ran out of the alley and through the school parking lot. "First I see them in the woods, and now they show up at my school? Who let them in? Did anyone try to stop them? What are they, above the law?! *What is going on?*"

"They're part of the mystery," Kid Kaiju said. "I

don't know who they are or who they're working for. But I know they have something to do with Gorgilla. Despite what you might think, he's really not a monster. He needs our help."

The kids ran through the parking lot, barely managing to avoid smacking right into the parked cars. They skidded to a stop on the gravel surface as they hit a tall wire fence. Kid Kaiju glanced over his shoulder to see if they were still being followed.

He saw the people in white suits run out from the alley. The mop had slowed them down, but only a little.

Kid Kaiju turned back to Amrita and said, "You better cl—"

Before Kid Kaiju could even finish, he saw that Amrita had already climbed up the fence; she was now on the other side, and dropping to the ground. She hit the dirt on all fours, like a cat.

"Well?" she said, staring at Kid Kaiju. "What are you waiting for? Are we gonna save Gorgilla or not? Come on!"

Without another word, Kid Kaiju got to the top

of the fence, and then jumped off. Or maybe he fell off. It was somewhere in between a jump and a fall. It was decidedly ungraceful, is what it was. He quickly got up off the dirt as Amrita grabbed his arm, pulling him.

"If you came here to help me, why is it that I'm the one helping you?" Amrita asked.

"Well, I mean, I—" Kid Kaiju stammered.

"I'm kidding," Amrita said with a smile.

They ran off down the street as the people in white hit the fence.

"Get the van!" one of them shouted. "Don't let them get away!"

CHAPTER 14

AMRITA AND KID KAIJU were running through someone's backyard, trying to put as much distance between themselves and the people in white as possible.

"Where are we heading?" Amrita asked as she jumped over a lawn chair. They ran past the house and onto the front lawn.

Kid Kaiju took quick, shallow breaths as he ran. "I think you know where we need to go," he said.

"The woods," Amrita replied.

"The woods," Kid Kaiju said.

They left the front yard and ran across the street. That's when Amrita saw it.

The white van.

It rounded a corner and sped up after them. If they stayed on the streets, Amrita thought, then they were as good as caught. There was no way they could outrun a van. But if they could stick to the backyards, places the van couldn't go, maybe they would have a prayer of getting through town. Maybe, just maybe, they could make it to the woods without getting caught.

Where's the Falcon when you need him? Amrita thought.

They bolted from the street and into another yard. The white van pulled up just as the kids raced behind a gray house.

"Unit Five to Unit Six," said a voice Amrita could hear from behind them. "They're coming your way."

Wait, she thought. *Coming WHOSE way? What does THAT mean?*

Amrita didn't have much time to think about it before a pair of powerful hands grabbed her.

◦ ◦ ◦

"Let go of me!" Amrita shouted.

She looked up and saw two people in white suits standing in front of her, while another held her from behind. Amrita struggled, but the person holding her had an iron grip. No matter how much she squirmed, or stomped on his feet, it was clear she wasn't going anywhere.

"You're coming with us for questioning," said one of the white suits.

"For questioning? I should be asking the questions!" Amrita shot back. "Like, what are you doing kidnapping a kid, for starters?"

"You're not being kidnapped," said the white suit. "We're taking you in for questioning. We've already notified your parents. You'll be able to talk with them soon."

Amrita knew that was a lie. There was no way her dad would have let that happen.

As she continued to struggle, the people in white suits started pulling her backward, taking her back across the front lawn and toward the white van parked in the street out front. While they were pulling her, Amrita noticed something else.

Where was Kid Kaiju?

Just a minute before he was there with Amrita, right next to her, as they were running through the yard. Now he had mysteriously disappeared. In fact, there was no sign of him at all! *He got me into this mess*, Amrita thought, *and then he just up and leaves? How are we gonna save Gorgilla when we can't even save ourselves?*

Out front, the people in white opened the back doors of the white van. Amrita tried to brace herself against the door, but she was shoved inside. Before she could jump out, the doors slammed shut. That was it. Game over. She had been caught by the bad guys. Now she was a prisoner of the weirdos in white.

I'm still gonna report everything I see, Amrita said to herself, as she heard the people in white suits get inside the van. *Talk about a big scoop—forget processed cheese food. This is gonna be the story that puts me on the map!*

The van drove off down the street. Amrita was

scared, sure. And she was super angry at Kid Kaiju for running off on her like that. What was he thinking? But deep down, Amrita was a reporter. She was hungry for a story, and this was a doozy.

The white van rumbled down the road, and

BUMP!

"Pothole," Amrita said, shaking her head, as the van went down and bounced up sharply.

Then there was another loud . . .

BUMP!

The van bounced on the pavement and went up in the air again.

Amrita waited for another big bump as the van hit the ground again. And she kept waiting. The bump never came. It felt like the van was still going up. But how was that even possible?

Suddenly, Amrita's world seemed to go topsy-turvy, and the back doors of the van became the floor. Amrita slammed against them with a resounding thud. She looked out the tinted windows, only to see the street below her.

They were in the air! Like, really in the air! They

were hovering maybe five, ten feet above the street. What was holding them in the sky?

The van started to shake violently as, without warning, Amrita found herself bouncing against the doors again and again, until the back doors at last popped open. Amrita slid right out of the van and landed on the pavement below with a smack.

Dizzy, she looked up. Her mouth opened wide. She was transfixed.

Amrita saw an enormous creature holding the van in its massive claws.

CHAPTER 15

"**WHAT THE WHAT IS THAT?!**" Amrita shouted as she picked herself up off the street. Standing before her was a huge, hulking tiger, standing upright on two legs. So, not a tiger. But it sure looked like one. It had a spiked tail, and it let out a mighty roar as it shook the van. Amrita could feel the creature's hot breath. She should have been scared, but she wasn't. Shocked, yes. Surprised, absolutely. But scared? Not a bit.

From out of nowhere, Kid Kaiju appeared on the street. He was panting—he looked like he had just run a marathon.

"That," he said between deep breaths, "is Fireclaw!"

Fireclaw let out another roar. Whatever he was, he was standing there in the middle of the road, big as life. His two claws were clutching the white van, holding it in the air with impossible ease. *That thing . . . that thing must be stronger than Hulk and . . . a-a-and Falcon and Spider-Man! Put together!* she thought.

Inside the van, the people in white suits were yelling to one another, trying to escape. It was clear they hadn't expected anything like this to happen. They were pounding on the doors and windows, but nothing happened. Fireclaw's paws were keeping the doors shut tight. For good measure, the beast shook the van some more. It was almost like he was enjoying it!

Amrita looked around to get her bearings. They were a few miles away from school now, on the road that headed out of town. The only buildings around were a gas station to the right, and next to it, a donut shop.

"Better get rid of them, Fireclaw," Kid Kaiju said.

Amrita was still trying to take this all in. "Wait!

Get rid of them? You can't do that! That's murder!"
Amrita shouted. What had she gotten herself into?

Kid Kaiju laughed. "No one's gonna get hurt," he
said. "Fireclaw's one of the good guys." Then Amrita
saw Fireclaw carry the white van in his muscled
arms and deposit it on the roof of the donut shop.
The giant monster gave the van a squeeze for good
measure, crushing the metal so the doors wouldn't
open. The people in white suits were now trapped
inside their own van. They pressed their faces against
the windows, shouting. Amrita was glad she couldn't
hear what they were saying. It probably wasn't very
nice.

"Well played," Amrita said. Then she punched Kid
Kaiju on the arm. Hard.

"Ow! What was that for?!"

"What was that for? For running off! For leaving
me with those creeps! For letting me get captured!
For not telling me you had some kind of plan in
mind! For . . . for . . . for everything!"

"What was I supposed to do? Get captured with
you?" Kid Kaiju stumbled. "I had to get away so I

could summon Fireclaw. I brought him with me in case we needed his help . . . which we did!"

"And you couldn't have told me any of that earlier? Like, before the goon squad showed up?" Amrita said, fuming.

Kid Kaiju held up his hands. "What, I was going to tell you, 'Don't worry, I brought my own monster'? I mean, it's not like I could have just brought him to school with me. I think your teacher might have noticed if I showed up at your classroom door with a twenty-six-ton tiger."

Amrita smiled at the thought of Kid Kaiju walking into her classroom with a monster. Suddenly, her thoughts were interrupted by banging, coming from the van atop the roof of the donut shop. The people in white were hammering on the glass, kicking at the doors.

"We should get out of here," Amrita said. "Even if they can't get out of that van, I'm sure they already called their friends. I don't think we want to be around here when they show up."

"Then let's motor," Kid Kaiju said. He motioned to

Fireclaw, who moved next to the kids. With one of his massive paws, he grabbed Kid Kaiju and deposited him on his back.

"Whoa, whoa, whoa," Amrita said. She took a huge step back.

"What is it?" Kid Kaiju asked. "We have to go NOW, Amrita!"

"No, I get that. But just give my brain two seconds to register that a giant tiger man is going to pick me up in his big furry paw and put me on his back."

Fireclaw turned his head and looked at Amrita. He sniffed. It was almost like the beast was amused by her.

"Okay," she said, taking a deep breath. "I'm good, let's go." She motioned to Fireclaw, and he picked her up gently and placed her on his back. Amrita held on tight as she could.

And then the giant tiger ran down the road and headed toward the woods.

CHAPTER 16

IT'S BEEN A WEEK OF FIRSTS,

Amrita thought, as she started ticking off a mental checklist. It was the first week she'd ever encountered a giant monster, let alone two of them. It was the first week that she'd uncovered some weird operation going on outside her town. It was also the first week where she had been chased and captured by strange people in white suits. And it was also the first week where she'd ever come home late for dinner and gotten the speech to end all speeches from her dad. So, yeah. There were probably a whole lot more firsts, but those were the ones that stood out in Amrita's mind.

Oh! There was one more. It was the first time she had ever held on to the back of a giant tiger monster as it ran down a deserted road and into the nearby woods. That was *definitely* a first.

"How long is the big guy gonna keep running?" Amrita shouted over the sound of breaking tree branches as Fireclaw thundered through the woods.

"Why? Do you want him to stop?" Kid Kaiju replied.

Amrita shook her head. "No," she said. "This is a lot to take in." Fireclaw was starting to slow down as the forest became thicker. "And it's pretty scary, honestly."

Kid Kaiju turned to look at Amrita. "Yeah, I guess Fireclaw can be a little frightening, especially if you're not used to the whole monster thing."

Amrita laughed. "You think I'm scared of Fireclaw? Are you kidding? He's awesome!" she said. "It's all the other stuff that has me spooked. It's like some huge monster conspiracy is going on right outside my own town."

Kid Kaiju smiled. "Well, yeah, when you put it that way, I get it."

"How did you even find me?" Amrita asked. Just the act of asking one question like that brought out the reporter in her. She fixed her most serious gaze at Kid Kaiju. It was her reporter's look, designed to make a person spill their guts and tell the truth. Amrita had been working on it for months.

"That's a story for another time," Kid Kaiju said. "Let's just say that the minute you mentioned finding that government installation, I knew you were in trouble."

"I knew it!" Amrita exclaimed, loudly. It was so loud, it actually took Fireclaw by surprise, and he let out a gruff growl. "Sorry, big guy," Amrita said. "Didn't mean to startle you. But I knew it! I totally got you to tell me who's behind this! It's just like one of those movies where the government comes into a small town and does some kind of experiment and then everyone in the town turns into zombies!"

Kid Kaiju raised an eyebrow.

"Wait, that isn't what's going on here, is it?" Amrita asked.

"That is pretty much the exact opposite of what's going on here," Kid Kaiju said. "But I guess I should tell you everything I've found out so far."

About a half hour later, Fireclaw put down Amrita and Kid Kaiju. They were still in the woods, not very far from where Amrita had first spotted Gorgilla or whatever the big monster was called. Kid Kaiju took the big sketchbook he had clutched under his arm and opened it up to a page featuring a drawing of a large apelike beast.

"Gorgilla, I presume," Amrita said, staring at the sketch.

"Gorgilla," Kid Kaiju agreed. "They found him on an uncharted island years and years ago. No one's really sure when. The expedition that discovered him wanted to bring Gorgilla back to our country. Supposedly, one of the scientists on the expedition believed that Gorgilla should be left on the island, where he would be content."

"Sounds like a good guy," Amrita jumped in. "But

let me guess. The people in charge of the expedition had other ideas. They probably wanted to turn Gorgilla into some kind of weapon. Right?"

"What are you, some kind of reporter?" Kid Kaiju asked. "That's exactly what happened. More or less, at least from what I've been able to find out on *Tales to Astonish*. That weird place you ran into, that dome? And all those people in the white suits, they're all part of some big experiment that has to do with Gorgilla. I think they're training him."

"Training him?" Amrita asked. "Training him to do what?" She knew that every good reporter needed to ask the tough follow-up questions.

"I'm not sure," Kid Kaiju said, closing his sketchbook. He pulled out his cell phone. "But I think you were on the right track when you mentioned a weapon. What if Gorgilla was being trained as a military weapon? You know, to attack . . ."

"That's garbage!" Amrita said, jumping up. "Forcing an innocent thing like Gorgilla to hurt people? No way. We've got to help him."

"Absolutely," said Kid Kaiju. He looked at the way

Amrita was standing, as if she was prepared to go into battle right then and there. "We are gonna help him, that's why Fireclaw and I are here."

"I thought you were here to help me," Amrita said, teasing.

Kid Kaiju blushed. "Oh, yeah, definitely! I mean, sure, that's why I'm here. To help you!"

"Relax," Amrita said. "I'm down for this challenge. Let's find us a Gorgilla, and save him. It'll be the scoop of the century!"

Just then, Fireclaw swiveled his large head from side to side. He sniffed the air. Something was there with them.

There was the sound of snapping trees.

Fireclaw pushed Amrita and Kid Kaiju behind him.

At that precise moment, the "scoop of the century" burst through the trees!

CHAPTER 17

THE ~~AIR WAS~~ completely still. For a moment, no one was breathing. Not Amrita, not Kid Kaiju. *Not even Fireclaw*, Amrita thought.

Amrita had never seen anything like him before in her life. There he stood, living, breathing, chest barely even heaving from the exertion of uprooting two trees from the very ground before them.

Gorgilla.

Amrita figured he had to be at least twenty feet tall, probably more. He was covered from head to toe in brown fur, like a bear. He had a long tail that moved back and forth behind him, like it had a mind of its own. And then there were those eyes—the ones she had seen staring at her from the woods just the other day. She looked at those eyes and tried to see the feeling behind them. Was it anger? Fear? No . . . his eyes looked more . . . curious than anything.

Gorgilla grunted at the group. He snorted, baring his teeth a little.

"Gorgilla?" Amrita said. She was doing her best to remain calm, but inside, her reporter's instincts were screaming, *THE BIGGEST SCOOP OF ALL TIME IS STANDING RIGHT IN FRONT OF YOU, SO DON'T BLOW IT!*

"Don't make any sudden moves," Kid Kaiju whispered. "We're here to help Gorgilla, but he doesn't know it yet! We don't want him to react badly to anything we might do."

Amrita ignored Kid Kaiju and walked slowly around Fireclaw, and over to Gorgilla. She took small, careful steps, and was sure not to move too quickly. The enormous beast looked at the tiny girl and cocked his head to one side.

"Grrrraarrrrrrrr?" came the sound from his fanged

mouth. Was it Amrita's imagination, or was Gorgilla curious about her? The monster tilted his head again as he looked Amrita up and down.

"What did I say about not making any sudden moves?" Kid Kaiju said through clenched teeth. "I said DON'T make any, right?"

"Who moved suddenly?" Amrita said quietly. "That was practically slow motion. Besides, he's a big softie," Amrita added as she continued walking toward Gorgilla. "He knows I didn't try to hurt him the last time I saw him. And the same bad guys that are after him are after me, too. That makes us friends. Isn't that right, big guy?"

"Aarrrhrrrrrrggg," Gorgilla growled gently, almost as if in response to Amrita. The creature bent down on his haunches, staring at the girl. Amrita stared back into his huge eyes.

"What's the old saying? 'The enemy of my enemy is my friend,'" Amrita said. "And you could use all the friends you can get, I'll bet." There was something in the creature's eyes that got to Amrita. The way they looked at her. Like a person. Amrita raised her right hand and held it out in front of her.

Gorgilla shifted his weight and raised his right hand, too. The motion happened fast, and Amrita felt a slight breeze as Gorgilla's arm went up.

"Fireclaw, no!"

Fireclaw had moved forward, trying to put himself between Amrita and Gorgilla. He must have thought that Gorgilla was trying to harm Amrita! Fireclaw didn't make any move to attack, though. He was just trying to keep the kids safe. Just in case.

Of course, Gorgilla had absolutely no way of knowing that! In his monster mind, all he knew was that something big, something threatening was moving toward his new friend.

In one swift move, Gorgilla thumped his chest with his mighty fists, roared, and rushed at Fireclaw! Amrita dived out of the way, rolling on the ground, as the two titans faced off.

"Kid!" Amrita yelled. "Tell Fireclaw to back off! Gorgilla doesn't mean any harm! He just doesn't know you guys! He probably thinks Fireclaw is going to attack me!"

Kid Kaiju raised both his arms and tried his best to get Fireclaw to stand down. But by then, it was too late. Gorgilla swiped at Fireclaw with an enormous hand, striking the first blow.

A knock-down, drag-out monster meltdown had just started right before her eyes, and Amrita had a front-row seat!

CHAPTER 18

IT WAS A SIGHT that stretched the limits of believability: two giant monsters going toe-to-toe. It was amazing, frightening, and if she didn't get crushed or stepped on or otherwise smashed, it would be the biggest news story of Amrita's young career! She pulled out her cell phone to snap a picture.

"Get out of the way!"

The voice belonged to Kid Kaiju. He grabbed Amrita's left arm and gave her a hard yank, pulling her out of the way of Gorgilla's giant tail. The cell phone flew out of Amrita's hand, landing on the dirt.

Gorgilla's tail swiped the ground, heading right for Fireclaw's fur-covered feet.

WHUMP!

The tail collided with Fireclaw, and the tigerlike creature hit the ground, kicking dirt up into the air. The earth shuddered. It felt like a tremor! Gorgilla snarled at Fireclaw, opening his mouth and unleashing an angry roar. Fireclaw returned the roar in kind.

The tiger beast rose to his feet quickly and glared at his opponent. He looked at his paws for a moment, and fiery claws suddenly emerged from the backs of his hands. At least, that's what they looked like to Amrita. Blades of flame that seemed to grow right from Fireclaw's knuckles. "Whoa! Add that to this week of firsts," Amrita said. "Flaming claws? What else can this guy do?"

"Well, his name *is* Fireclaw," Kid Kaiju said, his eyes warily glued to the two monsters.

Amrita followed his gaze, furrowing her brow. "Oh, yeah. I guess that makes sense."

Gorgilla seemed to sense the fiery claws meant

danger, and backed off. But only a little. He raised both arms, ready to defend himself.

"We have to get them to stop fighting!" said Kid Kaiju urgently.

"That sounds great!" Amrita shouted. "You're the monster expert. Any ideas? Is there like a secret word we can use?"

"Just one," Kid Kaiju replied. "MOVE!"

Both kids jumped out of the way of a gnarled tree stump that Gorgilla had tossed at Fireclaw the way Amrita would have tossed a crumpled piece of paper into the recycling bin.

"Move. Move is good," Amrita said, rolling in the dirt to her feet. "But I think I might have another idea."

Without waiting for Kid Kaiju's response, Amrita ran right between the dueling monsters. As the behemoths circled each other, Amrita maneuvered behind Gorgilla. Summoning all her courage, she put a hand on the beast's leg, letting him know that she was there, right next to him.

Without any warning, Gorgilla stopped circling Fireclaw. He looked to his side and saw Amrita standing there. She smiled at the great monster. She stroked the fur on his leg, just like she would have pet a dog or a cat. She had to let Gorgilla know that she was okay—she was safe, and Fireclaw wasn't going to hurt her. Would he understand?

It was working! Gorgilla was calming down!

"I think he was just trying to protect me," Amrita said. "See? Now that he knows I'm safe, he's not attacking!"

Kid Kaiju scratched his head, smiling. He looked at Gorgilla and Amrita, then at Fireclaw. Fireclaw did exactly the same thing.

"What do you think, Fireclaw?" Kid Kaiju asked. "You guys gonna be friends, or what?"

Fireclaw huffed, letting out a purr-like sound. The fiery claws on the backs of each hand disappeared as quickly as they had come.

Amrita rubbed the soft fur on Gorgilla's leg and looked up at her new friend. She noticed something she hadn't seen before. Something on his back. It was small and circular and white—it stood out on his brown fur. How had she not noticed it before? It looked almost like a smoke alarm or something.

"What is that?" she asked.

"What's what?"

Amrita pointed at Gorgilla's back. "There's something on Gorgilla. . . ."

"Don't move a muscle!"

Amrita whirled around, only to see the people in white suits standing behind them. There were at least ten of them, not that there was time for Amrita to count them all. They were brandishing strange-looking weapons.

Gorgilla roared, angry. Fireclaw responded with his own bellowing roar. But by then, it was too late.

The people in the white suits fired their weapons right at Gorgilla and Fireclaw. Bolts of electricity arced from the weapons to both monsters. There was a burning smell in the air. The monsters were rooted to the spot, unable to move, as the electricity coursed through them. There was smoke everywhere.

It seemed like forever, but the whole thing

only took two seconds. In those two seconds, both Gorgilla and Fireclaw were knocked unconscious by the Taser weapons. Amrita ran to Gorgilla's side, Kid Kaiju to Fireclaw's. As far as they could tell, both creatures were still breathing.

One of the people in white walked over to Amrita.

"Kids," he said, "you are in a world of trouble." The man in white opened a vial in front of her, releasing a cloud of purple gas. Amrita's mouth dropped open in surprise.

Amrita's world went dark, and she fell asleep.

CHAPTER 19

REPORTERS ~~ARE TRAINED~~ to take in every single detail of their surroundings and remember them. They try to notice everything, so that when it comes time to write about their experiences, they can relate everything to their readers. Reporters need to be as accurate as possible. After all, they're the keepers of the truth.

So it was particularly frustrating for Amrita to wake up and find herself inside a large, blank, featureless white room. There were no details whatsoever. The walls were white. The floor was white. The ceiling was white. The door—if she could even figure out where the door was—was white, too. There was no furniture. No nothing.

There was just her and Kid Kaiju, who was asleep on the floor next to her. She noticed that his monster journal, the one he always kept with him, was missing.

As Amrita turned her head, she noticed there was something else in the room with them.

Rather, some*one* else.

A really, really old dude with a scraggly beard and white-blond hair was sitting on the floor, watching her and Kid Kaiju.

"Good, you're awake!" said the old man. "I was getting bored, sitting here all by myself."

"Who are you?" Amrita asked, questions bubbling out of her. "Where are we? Are we inside that big dome? Where's Gorgilla? And Fireclaw? Who are those jerks in the white suits?"

The old man stifled a laugh. "Nice to meet someone who's as curious as me. You must be a scientist!"

Amrita shook her head. "A reporter. Well, I want to be one, anyway. I'm the editor of my school paper. And I write all the stories."

"Good for you," the old man said. "Search for the truth and tell it like it is. Don't let anyone stop you from doing some good."

Amrita picked herself up off the floor and walked over to the old man. He was wearing gray pants, a gray short-sleeved shirt, and gray slippers.

"Who are you?" Amrita asked slowly. "And why are you here? Do you have anything to do with these weirdos?"

"That's the million-dollar question, isn't it?" the old man said. "Wait, do the kids still say that? Old men like me aren't really hip to the new lingo."

Amrita laughed, and the old man smiled.

"The name is Scotty. At least, that's what my friends used to call me. I was a scientist, an anthropologist. I was obsessed with discovering the missing link between humans and apes. Wild stuff, I know."

"No, it sounds fascinating," Amrita replied. She looked over her shoulder and saw that Kid Kaiju was still asleep.

"This was years ago. You weren't even born yet. I thought I had found it, on the island of Borneo. The missing link, I mean. So I mounted an expedition, you know, as you do," Scotty said. Amrita chuckled. "And do you know what we found on Borneo?"

"Gorgilla?" Amrita asked.

Scotty nodded. "Gorgilla, indeed. We also found dinosaurs. Not fossils, I'm talking real, live, Jurassic-style dinosaurs. One of them attacked our group. I thought we were goners. But Gorgilla jumped in and saved us."

"That's amazing," Amrita said, as Kid Kaiju slowly stirred. He must have been hit with the same purple sleeping gas that the people in white used on her, she thought.

"It was amazing. Unbelievable. Gorgilla was more than a missing link, more than some sensational scientific discovery. To me, he became a friend. Some members of our group didn't have the same feeling. They wanted to bring Gorgilla back to the United States. I said no. I thought it was wrong to remove Gorgilla from his home. He had lived there in peace for who knows how long. To take him away would just be cruel. I told our group that we needed to leave the island, never return, and never say a word to anyone about what we had found. We needed to protect Gorgilla from the outside world."

"So what happened? How did Gorgilla end up here?"

"Ah, the young gentleman wishes to join the conversation!" said Scotty. A groggy Kid Kaiju rubbed his bushy hair and stumbled over to join the two. He sat himself down next to Amrita.

"Yes, well, that is also a million-dollar question. Like I said before, some members of our little party thought that Gorgilla should come back with us. They thought we could 'learn' a lot from him. By 'learn,' they meant he could be used as a weapon. There are lots of terrible people in the world who would pay a great deal of money to harness Gorgilla's strength for their own evil purposes. So I was 'overruled,' and Gorgilla was captured. I stayed by his side. I knew what they were doing was wrong, but I guess I thought I could still help Gorgilla somehow. Protect him. Eventually the people in charge decided I might try something foolish . . . like freeing Gorgilla. That was a few weeks ago. Now I'm a captive, too."

"He didn't seem so captive," Amrita said. "I mean, he's been out roaming the woods, hasn't he?"

Scotty shook his head. "He's just as much a prisoner as I am. Let's just say they have Gorgilla on a very short leash."

The room was silent for a moment, then Scotty looked at Amrita. His lower lip trembled. He spoke again. "I see something in Gorgilla. He has a soul, you know. You can see it in his eyes. He's no one's weapon. He needs to be free."

Amrita thought about the times she had looked right into Gorgilla's eyes. She had seen the same thing. Scotty was right. The creature did have a soul. There was something good and kind about him. Right then and there, Amrita became more resolved than ever to help Gorgilla—and to help Scotty.

"So what are we going to do about it?" Amrita asked, clapping her hands. "Just sit here?"

Scotty smiled at Amrita, then looked at Kid Kaiju. "I don't believe we are. Are we, son?"

"Ah, no," Kid Kaiju replied. "No, we're not. But first we need to find a way out of here."

Scotty shook his head. "First, our young reporter needs to ask another question."

Amrita thought a moment. What was Scotty driving at? Then it hit her. The device on Gorgilla's back. The one she had discovered just before the people in white showed up.

"We saw something on Gorgilla's back. It looked like a smoke alarm or something," Amrita started. "Was that . . . some kind of—of tracking device or something? Is that how those goons were able to find us? Is that what you mean by having Gorgilla on a short leash?"

"Bingo!" Scotty said. "You sure ask the right

questions. That *was* a tracking device. These 'people in white,' as you call them, put that on Gorgilla to make sure he can never escape. As long as that device is stuck to him, he'll never truly be free."

"Who are these guys?" Amrita asked.

"I thought I knew who they were," Scotty said, sadly. "Some of them were my friends. A long time ago. I'm not sure who they work for, to be honest. For a long time, I thought they worked for the government. Maybe it's someone else? A.I.M.? Hydra? Who knows?"

Amrita knew all about A.I.M.—Advanced Idea Mechanics—and Hydra. Both were criminal organizations that had plagued heroes like the Avengers for years. Even if they weren't behind this, the idea that it was someone on their level was still pretty frightening.

"So that's our plan, then," Amrita said, turning to Kid Kaiju. "We have to free ourselves, then free Gorgilla and Fireclaw, and remove the tracking device from Gorgilla."

"And how are we going to do all that?" Scotty

asked. "Perhaps you haven't noticed, but we seem to be unfortunately imprisoned."

Amrita stared at Kid Kaiju. They both shrugged their shoulders. In unison, they said, "I have no idea."

CHAPTER 20

"**A GOOD REPORTER** is ready for any situation!"

"I haven't met many reporters in my time," Scotty said to Amrita, who was feeling her way with her fingertips around the walls. "But you seem like a good one. You sure ask the right questions."

"She's good enough that these goofs in white want to lock her up and throw away the key," Kid Kaiju said. He was trying to be funny and put up a brave front, but the truth was, he was worried. He was worried for his friend, Fireclaw. What was happening to him right now? What were these strangers doing to him? What about Gorgilla? Would they be able to escape and free him? And what about his own situation—what were he, Amrita, and Scotty going to do if they couldn't find a way out of their cell?

Amrita felt the walls with her fingertips, probing for any place that might feel like an indentation. She was looking for anything that could possibly be a door, since one wasn't visible. She supposed that maybe the people in white could have teleported them inside the cell. Then she immediately dismissed it. They'd have to be Inhumans or some kind of super human—people with incredible powers—to pull something like that off. Or Tony Stark, maybe.

"Find anything yet?" Kid Kaiju asked as he joined in the search, feeling the wall. Scotty did the same.

"Not yet. But there has to be a way in and out of here. They just don't want us to know what it is." Amrita kept moving her sensitive fingers along the walls. She looked at Scotty. "You've never seen a door? How do the guards come and go?"

Scotty shrugged. "I've never seen them. They pump some kind of sleep gas in here. When I wake up, there's food."

Amrita's brain went into overdrive. Scotty said he hadn't seen any guards the whole time he had been there. That meant that whoever put them in this room felt confident that they weren't going to find the way out. So the exit was definitely hidden. That meant they were on the right track.

"Search the floor, too! Maybe it isn't a door we're looking for!" Amrita said, excited.

There was no way of knowing how much time had passed in the featureless cell. It's not like there was a clock or anything. Amrita tried to check her cell phone, but it was dead. No power. It must have broken when she tried to snap the picture of Gorgilla and dropped it. There was no way of knowing how long it had been from Amrita's burst of excitement to the moment when Kid Kaiju had found it: a small section of the floor through which he felt air blowing.

"Over here!" he called. "I think I've got it!"

Amrita and Scotty ran over to Kid Kaiju and knelt down next to him. They put their hands above a section of the floor. It was white, just like everything else, but they could feel air blowing in!

Amrita put her hand on that part of the floor to touch it. Imagine her surprise when her hand didn't touch the floor at all . . . but went straight through it! The floor wasn't there at all. It was like a ghost, a mirage. Amrita gasped. So did the others.

"What is that?" Amrita exclaimed. "Some kind of—of hologram or something?"

Scotty rubbed his chin and put his hand "through" the floor, too. "I think that's exactly what it is," he said. "Ingenious."

"So what do we think?" Kid Kaiju said, looking at his cellmates. "Is this an exit? A trap? Or just something freaky?"

The three looked at one another and smiled.

"Exit, trap, or something freaky, what do we have to lose by seeing where it goes?" Amrita said. "Let's find out!"

CHAPTER 21

KID KAIJU AND SCOTTY held on to Amrita's arms, lowering her into the spot where the floor wasn't there. Her feet "disappeared" through the floor as they let her down, little by little. Each held on to one of her arms tight as they could.

"Don't let go," Scotty said.

"Don't worry," Amrita said, nervously. "And don't *you* let go until I tell you! If there's no bottom to this thing, I don't exactly feel like falling forever."

"You'd find the bottom eventually," Kid Kaiju said, laughing.

No one else laughed.

"Sorry," he said.

BOOF.

"Hold on!" Amrita called up. "My foot just touched something. . . . It's metal! Wait, I can see it—it's a hatch! You can let go of me now!"

Kid Kaiju and Scotty released Amrita's arms.

"Hey!" Amrita called up. "Kid! I found your sketchbook! They must have dropped it or something!"

It was only then that Kid Kaiju realized he didn't have his sketchbook with him! "Great!" he called down the hole.

He heard the sound of Amrita's laughter coming from below.

The hole in the floor was big enough for Amrita to wriggle through, but it wasn't big enough for both Kid Kaiju and Scotty to stick their heads inside and see what was going on, so they were left to listen. They heard the sound of metal grinding on metal, like something turning around and around.

"What's going on, Amrita?" Kid Kaiju said softly, trying not to attract any undue attention in case someone was listening in from below.

"The hatch has a big wheel on it—it must be the release! Just another couple of turns, and—"

CLANG!

"Ooooof!"

Amrita had fallen from the hatch onto the floor below. She had never been captured and held in a freaky prison cell before (add that to the week of firsts), but she thought this had to be one of the worst-designed prisons ever. *Whoever built this prison should have their prison-building license revoked,* Amrita thought.

Bruised and only slightly worse for the wear, Amrita picked herself up off the floor. She looked around. She was in a hallway, all white (of course), and there was no sign of the people in jumpsuits. Looking up at the ceiling, Amrita stared at the hatch she had just opened. Her eyes continued to flit back and forth, left and right, making sure that no one was coming in either direction.

"Come on down, the coast is clear!"

A second later, Kid Kaiju fell out of the hatch and

landed on the ground. Scotty followed right behind him. Amrita handed the sketchbook to Kid Kaiju, who smiled gratefully.

"Whoever designed that prison should have their prison-building license revoked," Scotty said, brushing himself off.

"That's exactly what I was thinking!" Amrita said.

"Great minds think alike," Scotty replied with a smile. "See? Scientists and reporters. Same thing!"

"Well, we're out," Kid Kaiju said, checking the hallway. "Where do we go from here, Scotty? Do you have any idea what the layout of this place is like?"

"Not that I've seen. But let's think. All the activity in this place is going to be centered around Gorgilla. So we just need to follow the signs and sounds of busy people."

There was silence as the group paused, listening for the sounds of activity.

"I think we should go this way," Amrita said, suddenly pointing to her left.

"Why?" Kid Kaiju asked.

Amrita walked down the hall a little and pointed

to a small sign with dark blue letters. "Because this sign says 'Project Gorgilla Holding Cell,' and it has an arrow under it pointing this way."

"That's a good reason," Kid Kaiju said, as the group took off in the direction of the holding cell.

CHAPTER 22

FOR A PLACE that was built to house a giant, twenty-five-foot-tall gorilla monster, the dome was surprisingly small inside. It took only a few minutes before Amrita, Kid Kaiju, and Scotty had made their way down the hall and come to a huge antechamber just outside the Project Gorgilla holding cell. The group huddled to one side of the antechamber doors.

"I hope it's not lost on anyone just how funny it is that they actually have a sign that says 'Project Gorgilla Holding Cell,'" Amrita whispered.

They sneaked a look inside the doors and saw

Gorgilla and Fireclaw lying down on the floor, right next to each other. Both appeared to be asleep or unconscious. Either way, they were down for the count. Each monster was being held to the floor by what looked like huge metal bracelets that had been clamped around their wrists and ankles. Amrita looked at Gorgilla and saw the creature's chest heaving up and down. A quick glance at Fireclaw revealed the same.

"Well, they're both breathing!" Amrita said. She looked at Kid Kaiju as a wave of relief seemed to cross his face.

"At least they're together" Kid Kaiju observed. "Now we just need to find a way to wake them both up and set them free."

"And get rid of *them*," Scotty said, pointing inside the room. Amrita and Kid Kaiju looked where Scotty was pointing, and saw "them." There had to be at least twenty or so of the people in white milling around both Gorgilla and Fireclaw. They held all kinds of scientific-looking instruments, technology of a sort that Amrita was sure wasn't purchased at a department store.

"What are they doing?" Amrita asked Scotty.

Scotty shook his head. "I'm not sure. They have to be running tests on them, I would guess. Trying to find out all they can. How they might control them."

"No one's controlling anyone," Kid Kaiju said. "We need to distract these goofs in white. Figure out a way to get them out of there, so we can get into that antechamber and free the big guys."

"I think I have a plan," Scotty said, rubbing his chin. "In just a few seconds, all of those 'goofs' are gonna come running out of the room. The moment they do, you go inside. Now, you'll have to find a way to wake up Gorgilla and Fireclaw, and release them from those shackles. I can't help you there. You won't have much time, either. Probably only a couple of minutes at best. So you'll have to work fast."

Amrita stared at Scotty. "Wait, what's going on?

What will you be doing? This plan sounds dangerous," she said.

"Is there any other kind of plan?" Scotty said, and winked at the kids.

"Hey! You goofs in white! Over here!" Scotty was now standing in the middle of the hallway, waving his hands and screaming.

Amrita and Kid Kaiju planted themselves against the wall next to the door, as low as they could go. Scotty had taken off down the hallway, running. Behind him, streaming out of the door, were the people in white.

"Get him!" shouted one.

"He's escaped!" said another. "He must not be allowed to leave the facility!"

"He must not be allowed to leave the facility"? Who talks like that? Amrita thought. *Who ARE these people?*

The people in white kept on coming, flowing out of the antechamber in pursuit of Scotty. The last person raced from the room. At last, there was no one else. The people in white were so single-minded in their pursuit of Scotty that they had failed to notice the two kids flattened out on the wall behind the door.

"Go, go, go!" Kid Kaiju said as he and Amrita scrambled off the floor and through the doors. There didn't seem to be anyone left inside the large featureless room. At last, they were all alone with Gorgilla and Fireclaw.

"Boy, these guys sure don't like to decorate," Amrita said as she took in her surroundings. Aside from the monsters on the floor and the scientific instruments the goons in white had left behind, the room looked nearly identical to the cell they had escaped from. She turned her attention from the room to Gorgilla.

"So, how *do* you wake up a monster?" Amrita asked hurriedly.

"Very carefully," Kid Kaiju responded.

"What, is that a joke?"

Kid Kaiju shook his head. He wasn't smiling. "No, I'm being deadly serious. Wake them up carefully;

they don't like waking up. You take Gorgilla, I've got Fireclaw."

Amrita had no idea what to do. When was the last time she had tried to wake up a sleeping monster? Her dad certainly didn't count. Walking over to Gorgilla, she started to gently stroke the fur on the side of his neck. The monster grumbled in his sleep and opened his gaping mouth, letting out a loud snort.

But he didn't wake up.

What am I going to do? Amrita thought. *We only have a couple of minutes, and it's going to take FOREVER to wake up Hairy here.*

"SEAL THE PERIMETER!" blared a voice over a loudspeaker. "SEAL THE PERIMETER!"

The voice startled both Amrita and Kid Kaiju. They looked up, and then they heard the wail of a horn—the loudest, most irritating horn you could possibly imagine. It was loud enough to wake the dead.

Or a couple of giant monsters . . .

CHAPTER 23

AMRITA DOUBTED she had ever moved so fast in her entire life. From the moment the horn blared, Gorgilla stirred, unleashing an angry roar. She flung herself backward, sliding across the floor and away from the grumpy monster.

"That solved the waking-up problem!" Amrita shouted to Kid Kaiju. He had done almost exactly the same thing as Amrita the moment Fireclaw woke up. They were now sitting next to each other, watching the irate monsters roaring, groaning, and pulling on the restraints that held them fast to the floor.

"What are we gonna do, Kid?" Amrita asked.

"Wait, why am I still calling you 'Kid'? Or 'Kid Kaiju'? I'm calling you Kei! From now on, you're Kei, and that's final!"

"Kei is fine," Kid Kaiju said. "We need to find the unlocking mechanism—some way of releasing the restraints so we can free the guys!"

But there didn't seem to be any sort of "unlocking mechanism" in the antechamber—in fact, there didn't seem to be much of *anything* in the antechamber, except the two monsters, Kid Kaiju, and Amrita. The kids looked at the instruments that the goons in white had dropped on the floor when they fled the room, chasing after Scotty. They had no idea what they were. And it didn't seem like a good idea to grab them and just start pressing buttons.

Braving Gorgilla's awful, bad attitude, Amrita raced to the monster's side. He roared at Amrita, but she did her best to ignore him. She examined the restraints that held him fast. They looked like they were made of solid metal, completely smooth on the outside. There were no bumps, no holes, nothing that looked like a keyhole.

The horn blared again. And another voice came over the loudspeaker: "SECURE GORGILLA! SECURE GORGILLA!"

"We're gonna have company in about two seconds," Kid Kaiju said. He was now examining Fireclaw's restraints. "There doesn't seem to be any way of opening these things!"

"HALT!"

Amrita and Kid Kaiju whipped around and saw a stream of people in white suits pouring in through the doors of the antechamber. They were all holding strange weapons, just like the people Amrita and Kid Kaiju had encountered in the woods earlier. They advanced on the kids, slowly and in huge numbers.

Had they come this far only to be captured again?

SNAP!

It was like something out of a comedy. Almost in unison, the people in white stopped dead in their tracks and craned their necks to look at the monsters. They all had the same deer-in-headlights look. The kind of look that said, *We are in for a world of hurt.*

The sight was pretty funny, Amrita had to admit. Or it would have been, if the situation weren't so dangerous.

The SNAP! was the sound of Gorgilla breaking free from one of his leg restraints. There was another

SNAP!—the metal restraint from his right wrist was gone. Gorgilla was very nearly free!

Then it was Fireclaw's turn. He managed to yank the restraint that held his left wrist right out of the ground. Grabbing the metal in his paw, he threw the restraint directly at the people in white. The huge hunk of metal hit the ground, scattering the goons in every direction.

The sound of metal restraints being snapped from the floor continued. As quickly as it started, it was over. Both Fireclaw and Gorgilla were free, upright, and angry.

Oh yes, they were *very* angry.

"H-halt!" said one of the people in white. Only this time, the guy didn't seem quite as confident as before. The small army still had their weapons, but they were backing away slowly, moving toward the entrance to the antechamber. In response, Gorgilla and Fireclaw started to move forward.

The people in white moved faster.

"I hate to burst your bubble," Amrita said to the

goons as they kept on retreating, "but I don't think either one of these guys is gonna be halting anytime soon."

"Stand your ground!" said another one of the people in white, trying to sound brave. The others looked at the person like he was out of his mind, but they obeyed. "Activate the sleep gas! Use your filters! See that the monsters are recaptured, and take the two prisoners back to their cell!"

"Sleeping gas?" Amrita shouted to Kid Kaiju.

That's when Amrita heard it—a loud sound, like a thousand helium balloons being inflated at once. But it wasn't helium balloons.

It was the sleeping gas.

The kids saw great puffy clouds of purple gas rolling into the room from vents that lined the floor. It must have been the same stuff they had used before to knock Amrita and Kid Kaiju unconscious. The people in white were all wearing their containment suits, so they would be immune to the effects of the sleeping gas. But Amrita, Kid Kaiju, Gorgilla, and

Fireclaw weren't so lucky. Even if they did manage to find a couple of white containment suits for her and Kid Kaiju, Amrita was pretty sure they didn't come in size MONSTER.

If they didn't leave, and leave now, it would all be over!

CHAPTER 25

AMRITA COVERED HER mouth with her hand, and Kid Kaiju did the same. The purple sleeping gas billowed into the antechamber, seeping up around their feet. At least they were prepared for it this time. They could cover their faces, which would help a little. But it wouldn't take long before she and Kid Kaiju would be overcome. Same with Fireclaw and Gorgilla.

Whatever they were going to do, they needed to do it right now.

Amrita saw that Gorgilla was already doing it. The great beast lunged toward the line of people in white, followed closely by Fireclaw. Huge, fur-covered limbs were swinging in every direction, pushing their enemies aside. In the relatively close quarters of the antechamber, the people in white were on top of one another. They couldn't fire their weapons at the monsters without hitting one another—that meant they were going to have to wait for the sleeping gas to do its thing.

On the other hand, neither Gorgilla nor Fireclaw needed any weapon to press their attack.

Gorgilla picked up one of the people in white before they could even react. The guy screamed a little scream, then said, "Oh man, oh man, oh man, please don't hurt me, please don't hurt me!"

The monster kept the conversation going by roaring directly in the guy's face. Amrita wasn't sure if the guy had peed in his pants or not, but she wanted to think he did. Gorgilla took the guy, then waved him around, blowing a cloud of purple sleeping gas away from the kids. Then he flung the goon like a bowling ball at some of the other people in white. They went down like a bunch of bowling pins.

"Strike!" Amrita yelled, quickly covering her mouth so she didn't accidentally gulp in any of the sleeping gas.

Meanwhile, Fireclaw was keeping the rest of the people in white at bay with his fiery claws. Brandishing them from the backs of his paws, Fireclaw swept at the ground around him, creating a semicircle of flame. The fire burned high and hot, and the people in white couldn't get through it.

The fire also had another effect—it was consuming the purple sleeping gas!

Overhead, the horn kept on blaring, and a voice came over the loudspeaker: "Sending reinforcements to the antechamber!"

"Reinforcements?" Amrita said, rolling her eyes. "Ugh, these guys need to lay off. Gorgilla! We gotta roll!"

The giant apelike monster whipped his tail around and turned his head to face Amrita. Had he recognized his name? Or just the sound of Amrita's voice? Either way, he seemed to respond to her.

"Fireclaw!" Kid Kaiju called, and the monster looked down at him. "Make an exit, now!"

As the people in white struggled to make their way around the wall of flame, Fireclaw ran toward the side of the antechamber. He sliced the fiery claws on his right paw through the wall. Then he sank the claws from his left paw into the wall, too. He did this several times, weakening the wall bit by bit.

Then Gorgilla came running. The beast ran at the wall, leading with his left shoulder, and plunged right into the spot where Fireclaw had been slashing.

If you ever wondered who would win in a fight between two giant monsters and a wall, we'll save you the trouble.

The wall loses.

Every. Time.

CHAPTER 26

THE WHITE WALL came tumbling down as Gorgilla shouldered his way through and spilled into the fresh night air. The hole he made was gigantic (naturally). The dome was now missing a good section of wall. Barely a second after Gorgilla had barged through the wall, Fireclaw emerged. He carried Amrita and Kid Kaiju in either paw, storming outside with a speed that belied his tremendous size. A trickle of purple sleeping gas could be seen seeping into the air outside.

"They've escaped!" cried one of the people in white, still inside the dome.

"These guys are masters of the obvious," Amrita said. "Are they even paying attention?"

"They'd make great reporters," Kid Kaiju joked.

"No kidding," Amrita said. "There's no way these guys work for A.I.M. or Hydra—they'd never hire people this dopey!"

It was a whirlwind. They had managed to escape from their holding cell, rescue Gorgilla and Fireclaw, and break free from the dome. Now, all they had to do was get away, and make sure that the people in white could never find Gorgilla again!

Something much easier said than done, considering that the moment Amrita and her friends escaped outside, they were surrounded.

Surrounded by an army of people in white. They stood their ground, leveling their strange weapons at the monsters.

"Knock them out!" said one of the people in white. "We can't allow Gorgilla and that new monster to escape!"

Fireclaw turned his furry head to look at Gorgilla.

Gorgilla returned the gaze. Was it a trick of the light, or did Amrita see Gorgilla actually smile?

The next thing Amrita knew, Gorgilla and Fireclaw charged right at the army of goons. Adding to her week of firsts, Amrita had never seen such a large group of people scatter so quickly in her life. The people in white dropped their weapons and ran every which way, falling all over themselves just trying to avoid becoming a permanent part of a monster footprint.

"Let's go!" Kid Kaiju shouted. He sprinted behind the monsters, and Amrita followed. Gorgilla and Fireclaw were heading straight into the woods in the distance.

"What about Scotty?" Amrita called out. There was so much commotion, she wasn't sure if he had heard her or not.

"He's a big boy, he can take care of himself!" Kid Kaiju yelled back. So he *had* heard.

Neither Amrita nor Kid Kaiju wasted any time looking behind them. If they had, they wouldn't have liked the sight. The people in white were surging toward them.

They were about fifty yards from the woods, escape in sight. Suddenly, a white van crossed their path, blocking their way. Amrita couldn't believe it. They couldn't get captured now!

The passenger door popped open. "Need a lift?" came a voice from the van.

It was Scotty, smiling, in the driver's seat. "Hop in!"

Amrita and Kid Kaiju dived inside the van and slammed the door shut. She looked out the window and saw the large group of goons in white rapidly approaching.

"Go go go!" Amrita called as the men in white raced toward the van. In the distance, she could see three white vans just like the one Scotty was driving. They were getting closer and closer.

Scotty hit the gas and the van lurched forward. The kids were thrown back into the seat.

"Seat belts!" Scotty called. "Safety first!"

Kid Kaiju suppressed a little laugh as he put on his

seat belt and said, "Safety saves sickness, suffering, and sadness." Amrita gave him a funny look as she clicked her seat belt in place.

"Just something my dad likes to say," Kid Kaiju said, smirking.

The van sped down the dirt road away from the dome and back to the main road. Passing through the woods on either side, Amrita thought she had caught sight of Gorgilla as he stormed away with Fireclaw.

The three white vans were in hot pursuit. Amrita looked through the back window and saw the other vans. They were pulling closer and closer.

"Um, Scotty? I don't want to tell you how to drive, but maybe we could go faster?" Amrita said.

"Yeah, like, as fast as this heap can possibly go?" Kid Kaiju added.

Scotty tilted his head. "Okay," he said. "Just remember, it's been a while since I drove, so it might be a bumpy ride."

Scotty put the gas pedal all the way to the floor, and the van tore off down the dirt road.

CHAPTER 27

THE WHITE VAN swerved from the dirt trail and onto the main road, kicking up a cloud of dust behind it. Amrita braced herself on the dashboard and floor with her feet and hands. It felt like the van was on two wheels! She took a quick glance out the back window and saw the other three white vans hot on their tail.

BUMP!

BUMP-BUMP!

BUMP!

"Are you TRYING to hit every pothole?" Amrita cried.

Scotty still had his foot all the way to the floor

and was struggling to keep control of the speeding van on the pothole-ridden street. With every hole, the van jerked upward, launching its occupants toward the van's ceiling. It was only their seat belts that prevented them from clocking their heads.

"I *did* say it's been a little while since I drove a car." Scotty chuckled. "How many potholes does this town have, anyway?"

"All of them," Amrita answered. "And just how long *has* it been since you drove a car?"

There was a moment of silence as Scotty thought. "Thirty years. Give or take."

Kid Kaiju slumped in his seat. "We are gonna die."

"Maybe not," Amrita replied. "Look!"

She pointed to the van's back window. Kid Kajiu turned around to see the white vans that had been following them were falling behind! Scotty was outrunning them! For the first time all night, Amrita allowed herself a little bit of hope that their plan might succeed.

As Scotty burned down the street, one of the white vans suddenly bounced up into the air. When it landed, the van began to skid out of control. *It must have hit a pothole and blown a tire!* Amrita thought.

"Bless you, Scotty!" Kid Kaiju screamed.

"Aye, Cap'n!" Scotty said. Both kids just stared at the scientist, who let out an embarrassed chuckle. "Sorry. I guess you guys never saw that show, huh?"

Amrita wasn't sure how long they had been driving. She and Kid Kaiju kept looking over their shoulders to see if the two remaining vans were still following them. *Just because you're paranoid doesn't mean they're not out to get you*, Amrita thought. One by one, the vans dropped out of sight, until at last there was no one following them.

"I think we finally lost them," Kid Kaiju said, relieved.

Scotty looked into the rearview mirror. "Sure seems like it!" he said. "Kids, I think we are in the clear!"

At once, everyone let out a deep sigh of relief, and sank back in their seats.

"Now we have to find Gorgilla and Fireclaw," Scotty said.

"I thought we might be able to use *this*," Amrita said. In her right hand, she held up what looked like a small flash drive, the kind used for computer data storage. It had a red light at its tip that was flashing rapidly.

"What's that?" Scotty asked.

"That," Amrita said, somewhat proudly, "is a gadget that will home in on Gorgilla's tracking device."

Scotty crinkled his brow. "How did you get that? When did you get that? And how did you even know what to get?"

"So many questions. I'm the reporter, remember?" Amrita said. "It was easy. When you made your little distraction back there, I saw the opportunity to do some quick recon. I noticed that only one person had this device on his belt. One very specific person. I recognized him from a few days ago when I saw the people in white cleaning up brush around the dome. He was the one who used his badge to get in, making him a high-ranking employee with top security clearance. It was then simple to deduce that he was the most likely person to be trusted with top secret information. And what's the most top secret-est information? Gorgilla's location. See? Easy."

"Amrita, you're a miracle worker," Kid Kaiju said.

Amrita smiled as the van rumbled down the road. "No," she said, looking at Kid Kaiju. "I'm a reporter."

CHAPTER 28

THEY HAD LEFT the van by the side of the road. As Amrita, Kid Kaiju, and Scotty walked away from the vehicle, they were all surprised to hear a loud POP! Amrita whipped her head back toward the car and saw that the back right tire had just blown out.

Then something metal dropped from the bottom of the van.

Was it the muffler?

That was followed by the front bumper, which fell to the ground.

In just a matter of seconds, their escape vehicle had basically self-destructed. It was now a big metal heap, and it wasn't going anywhere.

Scotty laughed so hard, Amrita thought he was going to choke.

"Are you okay?" She chuckled.

"Oh yeah," he said, still laughing. "I guess I shouldn't bother applying for a driver's license anytime soon. Boy, I sure gave that van a beating, didn't I?"

It was true! Scotty had made that white van do much more than it seemed capable of doing. It really was a miracle that the thing had lasted as long as it did, and didn't just break down in the middle of the chase.

"We better keep moving," Kid Kaiju said, looking at the tracking device in Scotty's hand. "I wouldn't just assume that those goons in white just gave up."

"Good point," Amrita said, and they ran into the nearby woods.

It was only a few minutes later that the red light on the tracking device had stopped blinking. It was now a solid red, which meant that Gorgilla had to be very close.

A soft growl let Amrita know just how close they were.

She peered into the trees in front of her, and saw those eyes. Gorgilla's eyes. They looked at Amrita, and she melted. Running ahead, she leaped at Gorgilla, grabbed the mighty beast's right leg, and gave it a big hug.

"You made it!" she shouted. Gorgilla growled softly in response.

Standing right next to Gorgilla was Fireclaw. Kid Kaiju ran over to his friend and gave him a big pat on his leg. Fireclaw let out a roar.

"The gang's all here," Kid Kaiju said. "Better take that homing device off of Gorgilla now. There, Fireclaw!" He pointed at the small smoke alarm–like device on the back of Gorgilla.

Fireclaw nodded, and using his paw, grabbed the device, ripping it free from Gorgilla's fur. Then

Fireclaw dropped it at Amrita's feet. She picked up the homing device and held it in her hands.

"This sure caused a lot of trouble," Amrita mused. "And it's my proof!"

"Proof?" Kid Kaiju asked.

"For my story! My scoop!" Amrita blurted out. "This is gonna be the biggest story of my newspaper career! Imagine what will happen when the world finds out about Gorgilla. Look out, world, here comes Amrita Lakhani! Hello, *Daily Bugle*!"

Kid Kaiju was silent as Amrita's thoughts raced. He didn't respond to Amrita, but tapped her on the shoulder gently. Amrita's daydream was broken. Kid Kaiju pointed at Gorgilla.

What Amrita saw was incredible. Scotty, without saying a word, approached Gorgilla. Man looked at monster, monster at man. Both seemed to tear up. Gorgilla reached down and picked up Scotty in his massive hands.

"Kei, what's going on?" Amrita whispered to Kid Kaiju.

"Old friends," Kid Kaiju whispered back. "Scotty hasn't seen Gorgilla in forever. But see? Gorgilla still remembers him."

Scotty gave Gorgilla a squeeze on his huge thumb. "I missed you, pal," he said, wiping away a tear. "I'm sorry for what they did to you. I'll never let anybody hurt you again."

Amrita watched as Scotty and Gorgilla sat there in silence. They just looked at each other, but their looks said everything.

CHAPTER 29

AMRITA STOOD, watching the reunion between Scotty and Gorgilla with a mix of joy and sadness. "I can't write the story, can I?" Amrita said to Kid Kaiju.

Kei looked at her, shaking his head. "No."

"If I tell the world about Gorgilla, he'll never know any peace. How could I do that to him? How could I do that to my friend?" She couldn't, was the answer.

Kid Kaiju put an arm around Amrita. "It's the right thing to do," he said. "Gorgilla will come with me and Fireclaw. I think they're best buds now anyway. I promise that Gorgilla will have a great home."

Amrita wiped a tear from her eye. "I can't imagine

him being any safer than with the monster man himself," Amrita said, chuckling. "But what about Scotty?"

"What about it, Scotty?" Kid Kaiju called up.

Looking down from Gorgilla's mighty hands, Scotty smiled. "The big guy and I have a lot of catching up to do," he said. "And I want to make good on my promise to protect him. If it's okay with you, I'd like to tag along!"

Kid Kaiju flashed a thumbs-up. "Okay by me! I think Gorgilla would love having an old friend keep him company!"

Gorgilla grunted, and the corners of his mouth turned upward. Was that a smile? Amrita wondered.

The sun was just starting to come up as Amrita said her good-byes to Gorgilla. She gave him one last big leg hug. Then the monster bent down, gently grabbed her with his right hand, and picked her up. He hugged her close to his right cheek.

"Now, you be good," Amrita mock-scolded.

"Don't make me have to come after you again."

Gorgilla growled and put Amrita back down on the ground. Then she turned to Fireclaw.

"And you," she said, pointing at Fireclaw. "You better keep an eye on my friend. I don't want to hear about you two getting into any fights or anything."

Fireclaw gave Amrita a gentle pat on the head with one of his paws.

Amrita walked over to Scotty and extended her hand. He took it, and they shook. "I'm glad I got to meet you," Amrita said. "Gorgilla's secret is safe with me."

Scotty smiled warmly. "I know it is," he answered. "And I expect to read your stories soon, reporter." Amrita grinned from ear to ear.

Gorgilla picked up Scotty, and the two headed off into the woods, toward the coming dawn. That left Amrita with Kid Kaiju and Fireclaw.

"What about those goons in white?" Amrita said.

"I know some people," Kid Kaiju replied. "I'll make a call."

He walked toward Fireclaw, and the tiger creature picked him up. "Keep in touch," Kid Kaiju said. "You're pretty good at this monster stuff."

"I just might be," Amrita said. "I'll see you on *Tales to Astonish*."

"I'm just one post away!" Kid Kaiju said, waving.

"Stay cool, Kei," Amrita said.

"You too, Amrita."

And just like that, Fireclaw and Kid Kaiju disappeared into the woods.

Amrita stayed for a while, listening to the sounds of heavy footsteps and breaking branches, until she couldn't hear them anymore. They were gone.

"Aw, man," Amrita said out loud, to no one. "Now I gotta walk all the way home."

CHAPTER 30

IT WAS JUST a couple of hours later that morning, and Amrita was back in the office of the school newspaper, busy as always. She was exhausted, tired beyond belief. Her feet were killing her. Her body was one big ACHE. She hadn't slept since the night before, and had just spent the last twelve hours being chased, getting captured, running from goons, and helping two monsters make their escape.

Amrita's dad was waiting for her on the sofa when she got home. He was even angrier than before, if that were possible. Amrita explained that she was studying at Courtney's house and lost track of time. Her dad knew she was lying but also knew that the more he tried to control Amrita, the more she would pull away from him. He was just happy she was home safe and sound.

Amrita's mind was racing with thoughts of Gorgilla, Fireclaw, Scotty, weird guys wearing white suits, and Kid Kaiju. Meeting the young monster master had been an incredible experience. Amrita didn't know how she would have survived her monstrous adventure without his help.

She was at the computer, working on the front page of the latest edition. There was a light knock on the door, and it opened quietly.

"Amrita, you're here earlier and earlier every day!"

It was Ms. Malloy.

"Ms. Malloy!" Amrita called out. "I am so glad you're here! I'm just setting the front page for the new edition. I think this is going to be my best story yet!"

Ms. Malloy opened her eyes wide. "Is that so? You mean, bigger than the processed-cheese scandal? Or

Gorgilla? Fantastic! Let me see what you have going on. . . ."

The teacher moved into the tiny office, sliding behind Amrita's chair. There was barely enough room for her to squat behind Amrita and see the computer screen. Ms. Malloy started to read silently, nodding her head slowly.

"'Pothole Panic! Streets Must Be Fixed,'" Ms. Malloy read out loud. Accompanying the article, there was a photograph of one of the huge potholes that plagued the streets, along with an image of the broken-down white van Amrita and her friends had driven to safety in. To Ms. Malloy's surprise, the story made no mention of monsters. There was nary a Gorgilla in sight!

"I'm impressed, Amrita," Ms. Malloy said, breaking out in a smile. "After that Gorgilla story, I wasn't quite sure if you were going to pursue serious journalism or creative fiction! I mean, you'd be good at either one. But this is great—sensational reporting! You've identified one of the biggest problems facing our town, and you're sounding the alarm. That's exactly what a good reporter should do. Point out the problems. Deliver the facts. You can be a real force for positive change, Amrita!"

Amrita blushed a little.

"Soon as we have this printed, I'm sending a copy to the mayor's office. I bet we'll see some action on those potholes after this!" With that, Ms. Malloy left the newspaper office.

Amrita smiled to herself. She was glad she made the decision not to write about Gorgilla. *It would have been an amazing story*, she thought. Writing a story about the menace of potholes wasn't even in the same class. But the price for writing about Gorgilla was too high. There was no way she could sacrifice her friend's peaceful existence.

Especially when almost everyone in town wouldn't even believe what had happened that night.

On the bus ride home, Amrita and Courtney held on tight. It was the usual:

BUMP!

BUMP!

"So, what happened?" Courtney babbled. "Tell me all about it! You went with that kid to the principal's office, but you never came back!"

"Oh, he uh . . . helped me with my front-page scoop!" Amrita couldn't wait to tell Courtney all about her incredible adventure with Kid Kaiju. But she didn't want the entire school bus to hear. She would wait until they were alone. Amrita knew Courtney was going to literally die when she told her about the monsters she had seen.

"The pothole story?" Courtney asked. "Man, that was good! Everyone in school is talking about it!"

"You're kidding me," Amrita said.

"I am NOT kidding you," Courtney replied. "Who hates these potholes more than everybody on this school bus? No one! And because of you, it looks like they might actually get fixed. No more concussions on the way to class!"

Amrita laughed at her friend's joke. "It feels good to help people," Amrita said.

But she wasn't thinking about the potholes.

She was thinking about Scotty and Gorgilla. They

were with Kid Kaiju and Fireclaw now. She hoped they'd be happy.

Amrita's life had changed so much since meeting her new friends. She remembered the awkward kid that had walked into her class that day. Kei. She would always be grateful to him. He was her first big step into the world of real-life Super Heroes. The world she had always desperately dreamed to be part of in New York City. Not to mention, he was also pretty cute. She couldn't deny that!

As Amrita looked out the window and into the woods, she couldn't help but miss Gorgilla. But she realized that if she ever wanted to see him again, all she'd have to do is visit talestoastonish.com and post a message for Kid Kaiju. For Kei.

BUMP!

EPILOGUE

THE SIGNAL from the tracking device was coming in stronger and stronger. A person in white was clutching the device with a gloved hand, staring at it, while another person drove the white van. They were rumbling down a bumpy road near some woods when she cried, "Here! The tracking device says Gorgilla must be here!"

Immediately, they pulled the white van over to the side of the deserted road. Opening the doors, the pair got out, and opened the back of the van. Four more people in white emerged, each carrying strange, heavy weapons in their arms.

They followed the woman with the tracking device down the road. Approaching quietly, carefully, the people in white weren't sure what they would find. And then they saw it. Plain as day, right in front of them.

A broken-down white van, about one hundred yards away.

"Be ready for anything," the woman said.

The people in white approached the van with caution. What had happened to the vehicle? One of the tires had blown out, and the front bumper was resting on the ground. A thin stream of steam escaped from the hood.

The woman peered inside the driver's side and looked at the steering wheel. Stuck to the middle of it was a small, round, white object that looked like a smoke alarm.

It was a homing device.

The homing device.

The homing device that had been placed on Gorgilla.

There was no sign of the enormous creature. Or,

for that matter, of the other one, Fireclaw. And the two kids and the old man were nowhere to be found, either. *Very smart*, the woman thought. *Ditch the van, remove the homing device from Gorgilla, and place it inside the van.*

"Search the perimeter!" she shouted. The people in white fanned out, looking in the woods.

"They're not going to find anything, are they?" said the driver.

The woman shook her head. "No," she said. "They're long gone."

The driver scratched the stubble on his chin. He looked up, squinting in the bright sun. "What about that other thing they had with them? It looked like something that had the DNA of a tiger and a . . . dragon." He shuddered at the memory.

The woman's icy stare never wavered from the dense tree line of the woods. "Gorgilla and that new monster are miles from here by now. And we need to leave. It's only a matter of time before the Avengers find us."

"The Avengers?" the driver asked. "What do we tell the Committee? Won't they be angry?"

"What do we tell them? We tell them that it's not a total loss," the woman said as she walked back to their van. "We still have the DNA samples. There will be *more* Gorgillas. . . ."

THE END?

MONSTERS UNLEASHED!

WHEN GIANT MONSTERS KNOWN AS LEVIATHONS START RAINING FROM THE SKY AND WREAKING HAVOC ALL OVER THE WORLD, IT IS UP TO THE HEROES OF EARTH TO STOP THEM. BUT EVEN WORKING TOGETHER, THE AVENGERS, CHAMPIONS, X-MEN GUARDIANS OF THE GALAXY, AND INHUMANS MIGHT BE UP AGAINST A THREAT TOO LARGE TO TACKLE. WAVE AFTER WAVE OF LEVIATHONS ATTACK, INTENT ON RAZING THE WORLD, AND IT SEEMS ONLY A MIRACLE CAN SAVE EARTH NOW...

MEANWHILE, ELSA BLOODSTONE TRACKS DOWN A PROPHECY ABOUT THE APOCALYPSE--AN APOCALYPSE THAT INVOLVES GIANT MONSTERS AND A "KING" TO RULE THEM. AND IN MISSOURI, A YOUNG BOY NAMED KEI KAWADE HAS A MYSTERIOUS CONNECTION TO THESE EPIC EVENTS...

CULLEN BUNN -- *WRITER*

GREG LAND -- *PENCILER*

JAY LEISTEN -- *INKER*

DAVID CURIEL -- *COLOR ARTIST*

VC's TRAVIS LANHAM -- *LETTERER*

GREG LAND WITH JAY LEISTEN AND FRANK D'ARMATA -- *COVER ART*

ARTHUR ADAMS WITH PETER STEIGERWALD; KIA ASAMIYA; GREG LAND; FRANCESCO FRANCAVILLA -- *VARIANTS*

JEFFREY VEREGGE -- *HIP-HOP VARIANT*

JEE-HYUNG LEE -- *MARVEL FUTURE FIGHT VARIANT*

JACK KIRBY, MIKE ROYER & PAUL MOUNTS WITH JOE FRONTIRRE -- *KIRBY 100TH ANNIVERSARY VARIANT*

CHRISTINA HARRINGTON -- *ASSISTANT EDITOR*   **MARK PANICCIA** -- *EDITOR*

AXEL ALONSO
EDITOR IN CHIEF

JOE QUESADA
CHIEF CREATIVE OFFICER

DAN BUCKLEY
PUBLISHER

ALAN FINE
EXECUTIVE PRODUCER

LET'S MAKE THIS THING *REGRET* CHOOSING EARTH AS A VACATION DESTINATION!

INITIAL ASSAULT RUN COMPLETE.

I'M AFRAID WE DIDN'T ALTER THE CREATURE'S COURSE *AT ALL.*

SASQUATCH.

THEN WE MAKE ANOTHER PASS!

HIT ITS FLANK AGAIN!

HOW LONG BEFORE WE'RE OUT OF TIME?

PUCK.